TRAPS

A Secret Lobster War

Glenn "Kirk" Kirkpatrick

TRAPS: A Secret Lobster War A Randy Born Adventure
Trilogy Christian Publishers
A Wholly Owned Subsidiary of Trinity Broadcasting Network
2442 Michelle Drive
Tustin, CA 92780

For information, address Trilogy Christian Publishing
Rights Department, 2442 Michelle Drive, Tustin, Ca 92780.
Trilogy Christian Publishing/ TBN and colophon are trademarks of Trinity Broadcasting Network.
For information about special discounts for bulk purchases, please contact Trilogy Christian Publishing.
Manufactured in the United States of America

10 9 8 7 6 5 4 3 2 1
Library of Congress Cataloging-in-Publication Data is available.
ISBN: 978-1-68556-050-8
ISBN: 978-1-68556-051-5

Dedication

Holy Spirit: I thank You for choosing me as co-author of Traps. I apologize for occasionally getting in the way.

Barbara: thank you for your love and giving over much of our together time for me to write.

Corrine Leau: I can never repay you for the time you took from finishing your novel *ripples*, to read and spend precious hours enthusiastically discussing my manuscript in depth.

Carol Bond Wagner: Thanks for your encouragement and your leading example of publishing your *God is Out to Get Us* series which also helped propel me to finish this book.

**"Like an ocean, life is deep,
but we are just floating on the surface."**

— Michael Bassey Johnson, Song of a Nature Lover

**"Listen, I tell you a mystery: We will not all sleep,
but we will all be changed—"**

— 1 Corinthians 15:51 New International Version

Faint weeping sounds emanate from the silhouette of a young pregnant woman who watches falling snow against the black night sky outside her window.

Nighttime is the hardest; when she's alone with thoughts of her past. She wipes her tears and draws her blonde hair back from her eyes with her delicate fingers. In the dull glow of the streetlamp she studies her hands. The once healthy glow of a tan has long since paled.

The greenish yellow sodium vapor flood lamp on top of the pole illuminates a flurry of swirling snowflakes in a cone shape shining down to the white blanketed street. The intricate individual crystals each follow their own path as they float, hover, and glide on gentle puffs of cold air.

She closes her eyes, forcing herself to meld this scene with joyful memories of home.

CHAPTER 1:
Home Port

Baitfish shimmer against the deep blue mound of a reef. The school pulses as one, glides a beat, then sparkles as it moves again in a loosely choreographed spiral.

The creatures scatter as a rope ascending from the depths divides them. The braided hemp drags a lobster trap up towards the silvery rippling surface. A bountiful haul of nine more traps follows behind, all joined in a daisy chain.

Amidst shouts and laughter, a crew of lobstermen empty these wooden cages of lobster, clean the slats with brushes, bait each with a piece of fish and toss the now empty string of prisons overboard to descend back to the bottom. Two buoys with flags mark the position of each group of traps; one at each end. The flags bear the two Thorman colors: purple and aquamarine blue.

On deck, John Thorman wears the weathered face of an old salt who was born on the ocean. His white hair falls out from under a broad-brimmed straw hat. His snowy beard establishes an air of authority. John's six-foot two inch athletically trim frame seals his dominating presence as undeniable. Most men at his age would step into retirement, but John never considers it; he loves lobster fishing and, conveniently for him, can't afford to retire. John grabs a full trap and bellows, "Looket this'en. It'll pay fo ta trip. The rest's gravy. A 1975 record!"

Erric Thorman smiles mischievously. John's son is in the prime of life. He's clean shaven with a shock of brown hair bleached lighter by the July sun. His visage radiates confidence. His face bears an almost permanent smile, and the harsh sun of the Florida Straits has deeply tanned his skin. "Which trap full is for Rod?" Erric teases with glee.

Sonny Bays joins in, "Will Rod will take them all, mon?"

Erric laughs heartily along with Catbait's cackle while John smiles and pretends to growl.

Sonny Bays, affectionally nicknamed "Catbait" by his few close buddies, fully inhabits his powerful stocky frame. His lined ebony face puts his age somewhere between adulthood and Methuselah. Although Sonny was born in the Bahamas, he's accepted by local-born "conchs" as a native.

Although Catbait speaks seldom, everyone listens. Many say it's because he's a straight shooter. A select few know the reason lies deeper.

John picks up the microphone of the Sonny Bays marine radio, "John to base. Mamie, you there? Over."

"Where else would I be, John? Over," Mamie teases from the ever-vigilant marine radio perched on a shelf in the kitchen section of the living room. Merriam Thorman, called “Mamie” by a wide circle of friends, heralds from Italian descent confirmed by her full head of dark curls and dancing brown eyes. Her bright smile echoes in the DNA she gave to their son, Erric. Mamie knows God created her to use His love to serve others.

John signs off, “I’ll be home at day-down. Right ‘bout the pink ‘a evening. Over.”

“I’ll be here. Out.” Mamie stirs a simmering pot, replaces the lid, takes off her apron and peers out the window at the open ocean. It’s what she does out of habit, just in case the boat is in sight. It’s not.

Her mind floats to rooftop platforms enclosed with railings in Key West. These architectural features called “widow walks” capitalize on romantic tales of wives pacing these high platforms while scanning the ocean for their seafaring husbands; too many of whom never return. Others claim salvage captains used widow walks to look for future business; ships in trouble.

A television blares from the living room of their small stilt house. Residents of the Keys never turn off their television or radios; the hot tubes drive away the salty moisture protecting the electronic soldier joints. This only delays the inevitable; the copper metal eventually corrodes into greenish dust.

Mamie pays little attention to the TV commercial,

which seems to play continuously. A large black man dressed in colorful print shirt and shorts uses his deeply sonorous voice to invite tourists to "Come to the Bahamas. Celebrate with us for a Goombay Summer." The actor draws out his base voice intonation, pronouncing the commercial festival in a Bahamian accent as Gooommmbay Sommmah.

The commercial dips to black and returns to the six O'clock news on the Miami CBS affiliate, WTVJ. Anchor Ralph Renick reads another headline, "A major announcement by the Bahamian Government stops lobster fishing in the Florida Straits. Reporter Fred Hammond has more."

Mamie halts her exit out the door and gives the TV her full attention.

Fred Hammond stands on a dock in the Miami River with lobster fishing boats in the background. "Yes, Ralph, just minutes ago, the Government of the Commonwealth of the Bahamas Islands declared the spiny lobster a creature of the continental shelf. What this means is that they claim all lobsters on their side of the Florida Straits."

Mamie, as is her habit when worried, whistles a tuneless and breathy non melody.

"Until today, Florida fishermen have set lobster traps twelve miles off the Bahamas in international waters. The Bahamians have declared that any U.S. lobster traps in this area are now their property."

Hammond pauses and looks over his shoulder at the lobster boats in the background, "Lobster fishermen here are angry. More later on this breaking story. For WTVJ News 4, this… is Fred Hammond."

On the Stillwell Fisheries pier just a short walk away, Rod Stillwell tests the lift he uses to haul catches from the boats. His radio buzzes with the same report, "No one has paid much attention to earlier reports that the Bahamians would take over these fishing waters…"

Rod Stillwell's usually stern countenance turns somber, and age lines in his face deepen with the news. His broad shoulders slump, making the outline of his powerful thick frame seem slightly more rounded in the fading light. Rod is a hard business owner operating with a mixture of street-smarts and native intelligence sharpened by hard-earned experience.

He pulls on his trimmed goatee and mustache, looks to his left at the Thorman property next door; a long pier with the house on stilts near the shoreline. He notes the family outboard tied up at the deep-water end. His eyes trace back along the pier to the small white slatted house topped with a sloped tin roof. Mamie emerges from the only door and walks the rest of the way along their pier to shore, turning left towards Stillwell Fisheries. She pauses momentarily, takes some deep breaths and presses both hands on her lower abdomen.

Mamie arrives at the dock and meets Rod's darkly serious eyes, "Yeah, I heard on the TV," she says quietly as if speaking of the dead. She looks out to sea checking the horizon. "God knows about it, too."

Rod turns off the radio, takes a breath to reorient his thoughts and nods, "Yup. Yup, He does."

Just a few hundred yards away a truck deposits a hitchhiker on U.S. 1 also known as The Overseas Highway at Conch Key. The passenger thanks the driver as he hauls out a large dirty duffel bag and shoulders it. Jack's long locks and full beard are almost neglected but just shy of grungy. He draws in a breath, stands straight to his full five feet ten inches of his wiry frame and heads toward the gulf side. The hesitant rhythm of his steps underlines his apprehension.

Back on the dock, Mamie and Rod both look seaward but still don't see the boat. Mamie's gaze drifts up to the elusive Florida rosy cumulus clouds made famous by Florida landscape painter A. E "Beanie" Backus. She remembers the almost mystical experience watching Beanie paint in his studio years ago. He built layer upon layer of paint with brushes and pallet knives, creating sparkling reflections of light on the leaves of Florida vegetation crowned by his impressionistic depiction of rare Florida clouds tinged pink with the setting sun. Backus has been declared a "State Treasure" and stands for the same in Mamie's heart.

Newlywed Mamie and John could only afford to buy one of Beanie's student's paintings; Harold Newton's "Moon Over the St. Lucie River" hangs in their living room. Newton is a member of "The Highwaymen" who park along Florida Highways and sell their paintings to tourists.

Lost in his own thoughts, Rod watches a Florida Sandhill Crane standing in the nearby shallows, his grey and white body motionless. The bird bends his long neck down and then, like the strike of a rattlesnake, thrusts his head into the water. He emerges victoriously, holding a small fish in his beak as the red feathers on his head shake dry with the flinching of his prey. Rod muses the bird is oblivious of the human politics of catching food.

Almost a hundred yards away, Jack throws his duffel down to sit on it near the end of a stack of lobster traps. He hides as he watches Mamie and Rod. The picturesque scene he takes in melts into nightmarish clips of his past: running through mangroves from federal agents; an abandoned body chain-sawed to hide identity; a dreaded sunrise seen through prison bars; snow dusted pines in icy mountains; a small crude cabin. Cold, hunger, and loneliness.

The *Sonny Bays* rounds the point in the fading light. Mamie would have clapped, but her knowledge of grave news weighted her spirit. Two familiar Brown Pelicans land on a couple of dock pylons and wait patiently for the leftover lobster bait which Catbait will eventually throw overboard.

As the boat approaches the dock with running lights on, Rod studies the cracked and peeling paint spelling out the craft's name on the wood planked bow: *Sonny Bays*. With a pang of sadness, he muses over the history of this aging thirty-five-foot workhorse. It's the only boat the Thormans have left.

The *Sonny Bays* was originally Catbait's boat, which he named after himself. Sonny had fallen on hard times, so John acquired it from Catbait with the promise of keeping the former owner onboard as crewmate.

Over time, the Thormans needed financial help. Rod stepped in with several emergency loans over the years, even helping finance Erric's two years at Florida Keys Junior College and the loss of a second boat. Now Stillwell practically owns The *Sonny Bays* and its traps, but he sits under heavy payments to the local bank. John sells his catches exclusively to Stillwell Fisheries out of love and loyalty to his generous friend.

John and Rod go way back and have saved each other's lives several times according to stories gilded with the passing of almost forty years. But somehow Rod Stillwell feels the score is not even between them. He owes his life to John.

Despite the gloomy news Rod keeps under wraps, he takes a breath and smiles at the crew. John light heartedly teases Rod, yelling out, "Hey, old timer!"

"You know what that makes you!" Rod rebuts.

John turns an openly loving gaze at his wife, "Hello beautiful. Unlike Rod here, you get prettier evr' time I look atcha."

"You've been at sea too long," Mamie teases.

Catbait whistles a few notes of the old TV series, *Dragnet*, as if John's truly in marital trouble. Everybody laughs, and as the merriment tapers off, Catbait finishes with his trademark cackle.

From his unseen vantage point, Jack smiles faintly at the familiar humor and stands but sits back heavily. He's not ready.

John directs Erric, "Com 'on now, son. Let's get this catch outta here." Erric and Catbait haul boxes onto the winch pallet. They've had a decent haul, which they froze onboard straight out of the sea.

John pretends to lay into Rod with mock sarcasm, "So, tell me how low is the goin' price today?"

Rod retorts, "It's lower than yesterday."

"Tarnation! That's what you said yesterday and day before that."

Behind his father's back, Erric lip-syncs their exact

words, which have been committed to memory against his will for years. Everybody knows what's going on except John.

"Yup, and last week, too," Rod agrees.

"So, I work harder and get less?" John asks.

"Well, it ain't no fish fry for me either. Been wearin' the same pair of jockeys for ten years."

Catbait cackles and adds, "Hey mon, is your underwear like mine? So ripe I have to run and catch e'm every morning?"

Mamie smiles at the replay of this same old groove these men have developed over the years. She treasures how masculine men communicate their love for each other.

Usually the banter runs through another chapter involving complaints about the size of catches compared to past years, but Rod feels weighted down inside. But the moment of revelation must wait a little longer.

Mamie senses Rod's reticence and volunteers the setting. "Hey, Rod and Sonny, come to dinner at our house. Let's celebrate your homecoming."

Rod quickly makes eye contact with Mamie. She subtly shakes her head to signal a "not yet" message. He smiles and nods affirmatively.

Catbait grins, "Thanks, Mamie. Wouldn't that be glorious?" He whistles a short fanfare.

Mamie scurries away to expand the dinner for the spontaneous dinner party.

Rod helps the men cart the weighed boxes to the fishery freezer saying to John, "We'll work out the money, later, okay?"

"Sure thing," John assures Rod.

"Gimme five and I'll be over. I know everybody's hungry."

Catbait tosses leftover bait fish into the harbor. The pair of pelicans dive into the water, scooping up the leftover treasures as the last of the crew leaves the dock.

Under the cover of darkness, Jack stands, shoulders his duffle and warily makes his way towards the Thorman home. He stops short to watch and gather his nerve. He absentmindedly pulls out and fingers a small shard of blue and white pottery from his pocket. Usually Jack's forever boyish face wears a charming and mischievous grin; but not tonight.

Rod knocks on the Thorman's door and enters to join in the confusion. Mamie hustles about tending to the stove, commandeering extra chairs and designating where each person will sit. A knock on the door startles them into silence.

"Who's there?" John calls out.

"It's me. Jack."

The collective group shares a frozen and bewildered look. It takes a moment for reality to return. Mamie breaks the silence by yelling, "Thank you, Lord. It's my baby!" She rushes to open the door and almost knocks Jack off his feet as she tackles him with a hug.

His delayed recognition surfacing, John bellows, "Son?"

The roomful surges to Jack and pulls him into the cozy gathering. Jack, dazed from the dramatic reception, has trouble taking it all in.

John's mood rises beyond jubilant. "Mamie, get out steaks. We gotta' celebrate!"

Mamie dutifully dashes to the freezer and pulls out steaks, then realizes that they're frozen. Chucking them into the sink with a loud clunk, she dashes away and to return with a short stool. John grabs the stool from her and pulls out his own empty chair and offers it to Jack. "Here, son. Here's the honor seat." A now emotionally overcome Jack obediently sits.

Mamie loads up a plate from the stove and shoves it almost into Jack's face with, "Sorry. It's only lobster. The steaks are frozen solid."

Catbait studies Erric, who slumps into his chair and glowers at Jack. Catbait cuts his eyes to Rod, who then follows Catbait's gaze to observe Erric. By now Erric blankly stares at his own empty plate.

Mamie pours a glass of deep red wine and hands it to Erric. "Eat your bread in happiness and drink your wine with a cheerful heart, Ecclesiastes."

Erric shifts his attention to his own empty wine glass. His anger boils over. Standing abruptly, he shouts at Jack, "Holy cow! What do you think you're doin'? You dance in here like nothing's happened! You don't belong here anymore!"

Rod catches Catbait's eye and nods his head towards the door. In his soothing baritone voice, Stillwell softly and firmly addresses the eldest son, "Hey, Erric, let's have a meetin' on the dock."

Seething, Erric visibly tries slowing his panting breath to calm down, but never takes his hateful gaze off his younger brother. As a personal gesture of rejection, Erric quickly turns his back and stomps out the door to join Rod and Catbait outside.

The summer moon sparkles on the rippling waters of the tiny Conch Keys on the Atlantic side. This serenity draws a deep contrast to the storm raging around the Thorman home.

<•{{{><

Everyone makes careful small talk around the cleared dinner table. Erric makes a point to avoid looking at Jack; as far as he's concerned, Jack doesn't exist.

Rod takes advantage of a conversational lull, "We got some important news today." He catches Mamie's eye, who nods in agreement.

John takes a stab at humor, "Don't tell me lobster prices tanked again."

"No. Worse. The Bahamians say their side of the straits are theirs. They own the lobsters and what traps are there now."

John rebuffs him, "No. They've been blowing that hot air for weeks. That'll never stick. Our government won't let it."

Mamie backs up Rod, "It's true, sweetheart. I heard it on channel four news."

"Well, it'll blow over soon," John asserts.

Rod counters, "The government says talking with the Bahamians takes time. Right now, the Bahamians say your traps are their traps."

John sputters, "No, they're mine. They can't take them."

"Starting tomorrow the Bahamians are confiscating all foreign traps in their waters."

John objects, "Well, what do we do?"

Rod settles back in his chair with arms crossed, "I don't think we have any choice."

John takes it all in while everyone else watches with silent respect.

Rod reasons with John, "Ya know, John, as kids we had good times… and we toughed it out playin' with the dark side, too." They nod at each other and both glance at the floor.

John speaks up, "We worked hard. We ev'n come back from that there '35 hurricane. Now we gotta do sompin' so as not to lose ev'r thin'."

Rod takes a deep breath and lets it out slowly, "Yup. I agree. Don't think we have a choice." He grimly concludes the conversation, "We better get to it before them Bahamians get organized."

CHAPTER 2:

Desperate Voyage

In the predawn darkness of Stillwell Fisheries dock a lone whistler warbles the theme song from the movie, *The High and the Mighty*. The melody nearly matches the languid rhythm of waves lapping the shore, which are punctuated by occasional seagull calls.

The black and white perception of night emerges into color as the sun breaks the watery horizon and finds Catbait sitting on the Stillwell Fisheries pier. He's whistling and feeding bait fish to a pride of cats, which mew and rub against his body. He earned his nickname from this treasured pleasure in the simple life he now leads.

John emerges from the house and makes his way next door to the *Sonny Bays* at Stillwell Fisheries. Jack catches up, "Hey, dad. I'd like to come and help."

"Sure, son. The extra help's good. Even though it might be a little crowded."

Rod greets the two at the dock, "John, I feel like we're in this together… all the way. Could I come aboard, captain?"

"Sure, partner."

The three climb aboard and turn to find Erric standing on the dock behind them. He's fixed on Jack.

John breaks the awkward silence, "Jump aboard, son. We need to git goin'."

Catbait appears and apologizes to John, "Look like the boat's full, mon. I'm slow. Dis old body just get in the way."

"Oh, well. If that's how you feel, Catbait. We'll b' back quick as we can."

Catbait nods his head gravely. The crew gets busy checking fuel, supplies, and then casts off lines. John senses something amiss with Catbait who still stares at him dolefully; his eyes, the deepest brown John has ever seen.

Catbait intones just above his breath, "Goodbye, John. Love ya, mon."

A warm wave of electricity flows through John's body. He can't decide what it signals, but he rules out fear. He's heard Catbait speak mysteries occasionally. Mamie attributes it to the Holy Spirit. John flows with the feeling, "See, ya, my friend."

Erric fires up the engine, pulls the craft away from the dock, and throttles up on course for open ocean. John takes a last look to see Catbait still standing, unmoving and looking at him.

<•{{{><

Land is nowhere in sight. The *Sonny Bays* crawls across a broad expanse of ocean beyond the midway mark between home port and the reefs off Andros Island; a little over fifty nautical miles.

The inboard cruises between seven and ten knots, pushing the bow through rising swells. White plumes of spray contrast against the navy-blue depths of the Gulf Stream.

John stands at the bow as if he's scanning the horizon, but he's lost in thought. He likens his mind to jugglers, who used to spin a half dozen several china plates balanced on top of sticks on the *Ed Sullivan Show*. Those performers ran frantically up and down the line to keep spinning and balancing as the audience watched breathlessly, expecting at any moment the crash of broken ceramic on the stage floor.

John prays out loud, "Lord, what do I do right now?"

The still small voice answers, and John takes action. He motions to Jack to join him in the wheelhouse. John leans back against the console to face Erric, who's at the helm and pulls Jack in to form a close circle.

"Boys, there's a lot a'goin' on. I don't know how we're gonna do it, but we will… I'm countin' on both of ya." John grasps them both in his arms and pulls them in tighter.

"I want ya both to listen good and listen hard." John looks at each son. "Just know I've oays loved ya… an'll never stop, you hear?"

John stops, bites his lip, and takes a moment to compose himself as a tear wells in his eye. "You two's brothers… the only one's ya got. You got a bad feelin'? Just toss it overboard."

John levels his gaze until they each return eye contact. "Now, shake on it, boys." Erric and Jack solemnly shake hands and John firmly slaps their backs, perhaps a little harder than is necessary.

John looks at Jack, "Far's I'm 'cerned, all's forgiven." Jack feels a flood of warmth that fights with guilt from the past. He flashes on an image of storm surf battering his boat to pieces on the rocks as he struggles to stay afloat. The bow painted with the boat name *Mamie* is the last to disappear in the frothy sea.

John sees Jack's glazed eyes "Son, what's goin' on?"

Jack comes around, "Oh, I have these… they're like nightmares. I get 'em in my sleep, too. I guess they're like flashbacks to ugly stuff that's happened."

"Like what?" Erric demands.

Jack's confused, "Hard to… can't do it, man." He rubs his lucky piece of pottery and then grips it… hard.

Erric turns away to hide his disgust. His heart of stone refuses to give an inch. He opens his mouth to speak but stops upon discovering a ship on the horizon. Could that be the Bahamians?

Captain Clifton Newberry grips the helm of the HMBS *Rolly Gray* one of four patrol boats serving the Royal Bahamas Defence Force. His neatly pressed, lightly tinted Khaki uniform contrasts sharply against his dark African ebony complexion. Newberry's six-foot two muscular body stands taunt, his jaw clenched, and eyes intense.

Newberry's ship draws close to the *Sonny Bays*; he picks up a microphone. "Hail, *Sonny Bays*. You have entered the restricted fishing waters of the Commonwealth of The Bahamas. Heave to for a boarding inspection."

Throttling down his engine, a scowling Erric obliges the demands of the Bahamian captain.

No one speaks as Newberry and two armed crewmen step aboard the *Sonny Bays*. Newberry stands erect with feet planted apart, looking like an impenetrable wall. "Where are your traps?"

"None on board," Jack blurts out a shade too defiantly. John and the rest of the crew shoot glances at Jack while Rod subtly shakes his head, signaling for Jack's silence.

"All foreign traps in these waters are property of Bahamas," Newberry declares.

Jack fumes, taking a couple of steps toward the Bahamians, "They're our traps, man." The Bahamians shift their hands to their weapons.

John reflexively bolts in Jack's direction, trying to head him off from a physical confrontation. The aging man moves quickly at his age and the rush of adrenaline to protect his son fuels his lightning-like reflex, but he's beyond his own control. John's foot catches the edge of the motor housing, causing him to pitch forward. His forehead crashes into the gunnel and he heavily falls face down onto the deck.

The Bahamians back up, Jack freezes in horror. Rod and Erric rush to John's side.

"You okay, buddy?" Rod inquires as he and Erric roll John over on his back.

Jack presses in, kneeling down with Rod and Erric as John speaks languidly, "I'm a little dazed…" Blood from his head wound flows freely, drooling onto his face. He looks like he was in a bar brawl. Another Bahamian crew member boards the *Sonny Bays* with a first aid kit in hand. The Bahamian sailor kneels next to the boys, offering a roll of gauze. Erric nods and unrolls some dressing, applying pressure to John's wound. Blood rapidly soaks the make-shift compress.

The brothers flank their father, who groggily asks, "Do you boys remember?"

"Remember what?" they whisper, almost in sync

but definitely in confusion.

"Found you two minnows fightin'… Jack, you were younger and littler, so I picked cha up and pulled you outt'a the playpen. Ya know, that'n made outta leftover traps. Then ya stuck your tongue out ach'er brother. That made Erric so mad, that he charged at us. Busted through all the wooden slats."

The brothers steal a quick glance at each other. The familiar story usually brings smiles and laughter. Today's telling casts a mood of deathly seriousness.

"Erric, you're brothers. Can't change that. Can't help but love each other in the end." John looks at Jack and then Erric, "Ya hear?"

The brothers solemnly nod their affirmations to their father as his head wound soaks another wad of gauze and blood oozes onto the deck. John's gaze drifts past the faces of his sons to rest on the boat mast, which is also a simple marine radio antenna. A single metal wire runs from the mast base up and over the end of a cross member, over the mast top, back down over the other end of the crosspiece, and finally attaches to the other side of the mast on deck.

John's eyes focus on the geometry near the top. Ignoring the wire, he recognizes the shape made by the wooden mast and the right-angled support brace at the top.

It's a wooden cross.

The white underwater hull paint he slapped on it years ago is cracking and on the verge of peeling. To John's fading eyes this weathered cross standing high above the deck seems to glow brightly from within.

John quietly assures those around him, "It's alright. Just let God rule. I'll be fine." He slowly closes his eyes as if to rest. His face reflects peace. Over the next few moments, his heart slows and finally stops beating.

Jack slumps from his kneeling position to sitting back on the deck. Erric crouches with his hand on his father's heart. He stoically rises to his feet, pauses as if seeing his father for the last time and puts his hand on Rod's shoulder, "He's gone."

"What! No, no," a stunned Jack completely collapses on the deck. Rod straightens up, composes himself and asks Erric, "Is it okay if I radio the coast guard and deal with the Bahamians while you take care of Jack?" Erric nods a grim affirmation.

On board the U.S. Coast Guard Cutter Intrepid, Captain Robert Pembroke stands at the wheel. Military discipline keeps Pembroke's slim, six-foot frame erect and alert. His clipped sandy blonde hair complements his reddened freckled face. At first Conchs think his Nordic DNA is out of place in the Florida Keys, but weren't Vikings formidable sailors in ancient times?

The radio blares Rod Stillwell's shouted voice, "The

Sonny Bays to U.S. Coast Guard Cutter *Intrepid*. Over." Pembroke knows Rod's desperate tone of voice might concern their mutual longtime friend, John Thorman.

"This is the *Intrepid*. Go ahead, *Sonny Bays*. Over." Captain Pembroke scans the horizon and glances at the radar; his first mate closely monitors the screen for signs of the *Sonny Bays*.

Rod lapses into a casual but serious conversational tone, "Pembroke. That you?"

"Yeah. Stillwell?"

"Sure is, Bob. Sad news. John Thorman died a few minutes ago."

A moment of excruciating silence overtakes the two men. Their private thoughts run in parallel, reinforcing their shared past years. Pembroke struggles through a suddenly husky voice, "I'm very sorry. It's a loss for all of us."

"Yup. It's a shock to us, too," Rod nearly whispers.

Pembroke forces himself back into military mode, "I think it would it be a good idea for us to rendezvous. We'll do a basic investigation, officially engage with the Bahamians, and take John to the sheriff's office. The family can follow up. See if that's okay. Over."

Rod peers to the horizon, "Will do. I think I've spotted you."

"Yes, we have you on our radar. Out."

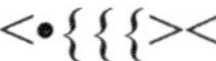

Fred Hammond appears on television doing a standup on a dock with the open ocean in the background. "The lobster war between Florida lobster fishermen and the Bahamian government heated up today with a human casualty. An accident during a boarding inspection by the Bahamian Coast Guard took the life of John Thorman, a well-respected lobster fisherman in the Florida Keys. He is survived by his wife and two sons. There's a memorial service at 10:00 a.m, tomorrow. For WTVJ News, this … is Fred Hammond."

CHAPTER 3:
The TV People

A white Chevrolet Impala with a black vinyl roof circles the sandy, shelled roads of Conch Key. Mamie stands outside her house and makes out the black stencil of the WTVJ-4 News logo on the car door. She walks to Rod's house while waving to the two men in the car and pointing to their mutual destination.

Mamie knocks on Rod's door and shouts, "Put your teeth in Rod. The TV people are here."

The driver of the news car, Randy Born, pulls up in front of the Stillwell home. Born, 26, hails from the lakes of central Florida, but after graduating from Stetson University in DeLand, he settled down in South Florida. His blue eyes belay intelligence both from his education and his profession as a news cameraman on the streets of Miami. "Do you want me to suit up?" he asks his passenger.

Fred Hammond turns to look at Born, noticing beads of sweat on his tanned face his longish wavey hair has almost kinked in the sweltering humidity. "Not just yet. Let me get the lay of the land. It could be a bust."

Fred Hammond is one of those people who never sweats. He's literally a cool character. His dark skin and deep brown eyes complement his slight but confident smile. Born and raised by his Lebanese parents in Miami, he acquired street smarts by living life on the edge as a bouncer in a down and dirty night club. Although his stature is a less than imposing five foot ten, Fred levels the playing field with speed and cunning.

"Hi, there. I'm Fred Hammond. Are you Rod Stillwell?"

Rod smiles and nods in recognition, "Yeah. You're Channel 4."

Fred smiles broadly to acknowledge Rod's reference to his on-air sign off, "Yeah. This is me." They both grin and shake hands.

"What can I do for ya?" Rod offers.

"Heard your name mentioned a lot. Just want to touch base with the lobster fishermen here to see what they think and what they're planning."

"Well, the funeral's in a few minutes," Stillwell politely objects.

Ever on the police beat mostly dealing with murders, Hammond wonders out loud, "So soon?"

"Yeah, John wanted his ashes scattered in the Gulf Stream."

Fred realizes he might have appeared insensitive, "Sorry, that may have been off base. Could we set up a meet sometime soon?"

Rod pulls at his beard. Wanting to demonstrate good faith, he offers, "I don't wanna talk for everybody. How about you come to the Union meeting tonight? It'll be right there." Rod points to Stillwell Fisheries a stone's throw away. "Those guys all like to talk… or shout… dependin'."

"Good, idea, Rod. Thanks. I like the way you think. Here's my card. Call me if you think we can help each other."

Rod studies the card, straightens his moustache between his thumb and forefinger, nods and then offers to shake Fred's hand, "That's a deal."

<•{{{><

Locals stuff the church sanctuary to overflowing. Pastor Mike Kenyon is both pleased at the crowd and saddened by the occasion. He knows John Thorman deserves this full and loving turnout memorial but wishes Sunday mornings could be like this.

Pastor Kenyon knows through tough experience, that fishing for men proves problematic in the Keys. Too many males suffer from what's called "Keys disease." The classic symptoms manifest as guzzling alcohol, chasing ladies, and forever fishing… at the expense of the rest of their lives.

Pastor Kenyon silently prays away this and the rest of

his personal life pains. His plain and meek face radiates kindness with a subtle, warm smile. He stands from his chair on the platform and removes his spectacles to polish them with a handkerchief, daubs his teary eyes, and replaces his glasses on his head. A touch with his finger adjusts his specs tightly on his nose. He's as ready as he'll ever be. The crowd shifts from hushed whispers to absolute silence.

Kenyon steps to the pulpit to gaze at the crowd for a moment. "John Thorman. John Thorman. He was a man among men. Now he's a spirit among angels."

Erric turns to survey the congregants in the sanctuary behind him. He spots the guy he's seen on the news and another man next to him. His eyes shift to the double doors, opening quietly and slowly. Captain Pembroke, out of uniform, pokes his head in the door. He scans the room, enters, and walks to the far back wall with a woman in tow. The woman turns to face the pulpit and draws her blonde hair back from her eyes with her fingers.

Erric stares in disbelief and asks himself could that be Katherine Stillwell?

He's stunned. A part of him is thankful for the numbness he feels because his already turbulent emotions now are brimming in his eyes and in danger of overflowing. Deep sadness for his deceased father mix with years of joyful memories with Katherine. Soon the painful question he's tried to forget over the years seems to ring loudly in his ears. *Why Katherine? Why?*

Adding to his confusion, Erric wonders, what's she doing with Pembroke?

The funeral blurs by. Erric comes back to consciousness realizing the service is over. He scans the crowd, but Pembroke and Katherine have disappeared along with her father, Rod Stillwell.

<•{{{><

Jack pulls into Goodsprings Bar & Grill, which sits on a spit of land at the southern-most tip of Marathon Key. Jack muses it has changed little on the outside except for some weathering. He enters and stops dead. Even he notices the remodeling; opposing walls painted complementary aqua and neon pink an homage to Miami Vice. Imitation Tiffany lamps hang over the tables.

A shout breaks Jack's near stupor, "Is that Jack Thorman?" It's flashy new decorations but same old crowd. The commercial lobster fishermen have gathered after the service.

Another voice calls out, "Hey, Jack. What are you doing down in the Keys?"

A third man speaks up from the back, "Welcome back to The Conch Republic."

Jack smiles, shakes his head, and shrugs to this string of

comments. The door behind opens and gently nudges him aside. The silhouette of a tall man ducks to miss the door frame as he enters. His square shaped head and matching jaws connect with a short neck to his powerfully bulky body. Its Deputy Sheriff Larry Beeker.

Jack turns to face the newcomer, “Yeti?”

“Jack?”

They embrace, slapping each other on the back. “Yeti!” Larry laughs. “I’d forgotten you called me that.”

“You look good, Yeti. What’s with the uniform?”

“I’m a sheriff’s deputy, now. Gave up fishin’.”

Jack’s face falls but he quickly recovers with a weak smile, “Far out.”

Larry laughs, “Don’t worry, captain. Statute of limitations ran out a while back. Hey, sorry about jumping ship after all that happened.”

Slightly numbed, Jack searches for words as if they had fallen on the floor. He flashes on the memory of the Mamie… sinking.

“Sorry to hear about your dad,” Larry continues. Jack bites his lip and nods.

“Your mom’s okay, right?”

Jack meekly replies, “Yeah, she’s fine.”

Larry looks past Jack, smiles, and nods. “Okay, I’ve checked in. Gotta get back to patrolling. See you around.”

“It’s good seeing you, Yeti,” Jack manages to say good-naturedly. He watches Larry go out the door and then turns around to see who Larry checked in with to meet eyes with Jean Goodsprings. The owner’s daughter wipes down the bar and slyly studies him. Jack nearly charges at her, “Jean!”

The raised platform on which Jean “Jazzie” Goodsprings stands behind the bar belies her diminutive five-foot two-inch figure. Her jet-black hair sports a pixie cut with slight bouffant on top to offset her height. She wears what has become her trademark garb: cut off jean shorts with a white buttoned short-sleeved blouse. Jazzie customizes her look by leaving a few buttons open and tying the front shirt tails in a knot, revealing a bare midriff and a bit of cleavage. She smiles whimsically and lets out a languid sigh, “It’s Jazzie, now.”

Jack admires afresh her elfin face and flashing black eyes. “Jazzie?”

“Yeah, you know daddy died in ’72 and left me this place.”

“I’m sorry to hear that.”

Jazzie ignores him, “I decided to jazz the place up a bit. That’s how I got the nickname.”

"I guess you like it, huh?"

"Better'n my legal name. Did'cha know that I was named after a tiny place called Jean in the Nevada desert? It's next to Goodsprings, daddy's family hometown."

"Didn't know that. You got any other fascinating secrets you want to share with this guy? I got plenty of time."

Jazzie smiles coyly, "Jack, you haven't changed much, have you?"

"Haven't changed how I feel about you."

Jazzie levels her eyes with his, "Jack, we were never really an item, now were we?"

Momentarily crushed, Jack recalls repressed scenes of Jean alternately teasing and then rejecting him. He wills himself to remember only his secret dreams. Out comes his ceramic remnant. Jack notes that his nervous habit puzzles Jazzie. He performs for her by manipulating the coin-like piece magically through the fingers of his right hand.

"Is that a piece of painted ivory?" Jazzie quizzes.

"No, it's chany."

Showing interest Jazzie continues, "I think I've heard of it…"

"Chany is a cross between china, you know, pieces plates and money. Kids find them and use 'em like play money. China… money… chany."

Still following the object as Jack juggles it between his digits, she asks, "So where does it come from?"

"Picked it up on a beach in St. Croix. There are a lot on the bottom of the harbor because in the old days imported china was taxed by weight."

Jazzie holds out her hand and Jack gives it to her.

Jack continues, "The ship's captain would order the men to throw broken pieces overboard before they weighed the rest for taxes."

She notes a partial design in blue adorns one side. Smooth, worn edges blur the once jagged fragment.

"This chany could also be left over from the slave rebellion when the islanders burned and looted the plantations of the rich." Jazzy nods and extends her hand to give the relic back. "That could actually be worth big bucks…" Jazzie jerks her hand back as if she wants to keep this treasure. Jack sees her eyes sparkle and loves it.

"How come?" she asks.

"I looked up from my bar drink somewhere in the islands and fell in love with a print of a painting on the wall by Paul Gauguine. He depicted south sea island fantasies of half nude native women in idyllic Pacific island settings. That fascination led me to the French Impressionists."

Jazzie emphatically points to the porcelain good luck charm in her hand, “Get on with it.”

“Do you know the French painter… Renoir? Two girls at a piano?” Jazzie slowly shakes her head, showing impatience. “The Dancer?” Jazzie pulls her head back and glares at him sideways, “Where are you getting all this?”

“I didn’t go to college, but I’ve had a lot of time to read books and meet astute people,” Jack assures her. Jazzie gives Jack the satisfaction of a little nod.

“Anyway, Renoir’s world famous and his works go for hundreds of thousands… maybe millions.”

“So?”

Jack puts on a playful air of superiority, “This guy, Renoir, apprenticed as a porcelain decorator in France. It could be, it just could be that he painted the plate that this scrap came from!”

Jazzie rolls her eyes and deposits the chany on the counter in front of Jack like it’s a piece of smelly garbage. Jack guffaws.

The door bursts open and Erric makes a dramatic entrance wearing his game face, “Go Hurricanes!”

The crowd raggedly but enthusiastically responds, “Go Hurricanes!”

“Hey, Trap. Sorry ‘bout your dad,” a voice in the crowd

sympathizes.

Erric looks groundward, "Yeah, it's hard." He's determined to let go of the present tragedy. Erric forces his mind back to playing football for Coral Shores High when he caught and tenaciously carried the football. He trapped it with both arms against his chest and never, ever fumbled. Hence his nickname, "Trap."

Erric raises his head, bursts into a brave grin, and points to his chest, "One of these days Trap is gonna return Don Shula's call and play for the Dolphins." The crowd laughs amidst a few claps.

Erric slides into the stool next to Jack.

"Hey, Trap, how about a beer?" Jazzie purrs.

Erric glances at her,"Yeah, Jazz. The usual."

"Me, too," Jack adds but gets no response.

The brothers each stare out the window at the water flowing through the cut between the keys. Jazzie slides Jack's beer at him and carefully places the other in front of Erric. The uptight silence between brothers crystalizes like old dynamite sticks sweating out crystals of nitroglycerin.

"Those thievin' Bahamians!" Jack blurts out startling Erric to reality.

"What?"

Jack spits it out, "They killed dad."

"No, idiot! It was an accident. Dad died trying to save you."

"An accident they caused," Jack seethes.

"Don't get your panties in a wad."

"Don't tell me what to do, man," Jack warns.

"I didn't tell you to take the Mamie and run drugs."

"Dad gave it to me."

Erric sighs deeply to calm down, "Only because you demanded it. Wanted your share now instead of waiting." Erric pauses before going for the kill, "It's like saying, 'I'm not gonna wait for you to die. I want it now!'"

Jack's sails go slack; there's no wind left. He stares forlornly into his beer, his lips pulled tight across his vexed face. The younger brother hides his shame. He says nothing and needs a lot.

Jazzie turns up the TV over the bar. Fred Hammond is doing a standup in front of Stillwell Fisheries, "That's right, Ralph. Reports still confirm that Bahamian gun boats still patrol what they call their exclusive lobster fishing grounds. The Bahamian Government threatens to arrest all crewmen and confiscate all boats. So far, the U.S. Government has not responded. Meanwhile, the Fishermen's Union will meet here later tonight to discuss the future of their livelihood. For WTVJ News this… is Fred Hammond."

CHAPTER 4:
Familiar Stranger

It's what photographers call "the magic hour" on Conch Key. About a half hour ago the sun dropped below the horizon; a narrow band of bright sky at the horizon bathes Stillwell Fisheries in a cool soft light. Warm light spills out the building doorway and illuminates the windows.

The painterly exterior belies the restless sounds emanating from the interior where angry union members pack the processing floor.

Javier Gonzales and a few other Cubans segregate near the back. Javier's dark eyes dart nervously across the crowd. His light brown complexion sparkles with dewy perspiration. Although on guard, Javier stands firmly in place next to the aisle while disregarding those passing by who pretend to accidentally bump into him and make ill-toned remarks, "Get out of our waters." "Go back to Miami." "Go back to Cuba."

Two portable quartz lights on stands blaze to life and bathe the room in a harsh glare. Everyone's attention is on Randy Born with a news film camera poised on his shoulder and Fred Hammond at his side.

Rod Stillwell steps up on a short stack of pallets which

serve as a meeting platform, "Evening, ladies." A few nervous guffaws break some tension in the room.

"There's lots to cover. Last meetin' was pretty simple. Darryl, you wanna read them minutes?"

Darryl Collier, a very short and wiry character, steps up on the short stack of pallets. A heckler shouts, "Hey, Darryl, stand up when you talk!" Light laughter echoes around the room. The crowd never completely quiets down.

Darryl pulls a small wad of blue-lined notebook paper from his shirt pocket, unfolds it, and peers at his penciled writing for a moment; almost as if he's never seen it before. His face relaxes with recognition. The men shift on their feet. Finally, Darryl takes a lungful of air and opens his mouth. The men brace themselves. "The minutes of the last meetin'," he declares.

Darryl's voice marks him as a notable character in the Keys. It sounds like air forced through a pipe, past a serious dent and across sandpaper. It's wheezy with random high-pitched whining sounds. To make hearing him even more of a challenge, Darryl can't seem to speak at a volume much more than a stage whisper. Someone remarked that Darryl's voice sounded like something just this side of a death rattle.

The gathering slowly inches forward and some old salts cock their heads to favor their best ear.

"Sounds good to me," Rod announces when Darryl

finishes. A few men suppress a chuckle. "Let's 'cept the minutes." Rod raises his hand and the rest follow suit.

"Now, as planned, we're goin' tuh deal with the federal fish traps ban," Rod forces himself to announce casually, but the room won't have it. This new federal regulation prohibits wire fish traps fishermen have used for years to catch fish to eat or bait lobster traps. By now the union membership mood rises past simmering distaste to a near boil.

"We got a special speaker from D.C." Rod nods at the back of the room where Captain Pembroke seems to have magically appeared.

All turn to see Pembroke in his Coast Guard dress whites, which seem to light up that dark area. There's confusion as if the gang thinks in unison, *what's Pembroke doing here?*

Pembroke nods to Rod and opens the door. Katherine Stillwell confidently strides in. She glows in her pleated white dress and white pumps topped by her stylish long blonde locks.

Erric fondly and painfully remembers how gracefully Katherine walks. Her head floats on an even keel without bobbing up and down. Her movements seemed played back from a movie projected in elegant slow motion as she navigates to the front of the meeting.

The red-faced fishermen spoil for a scrap but stand silent, shocked, and confused. Veins in their necks stand out throbbing with anger, but they can't fight a pretty, feminine woman… especially if she's Stillwell's long-lost daughter. The air turns a tint of blue with whispered swearing, both out of anger and in awe.

Erric, Jack, and Catbait stare in shock.

"Good evening, gentleman," Katherine's pleasingly smooth voice calms their angry hearts. "I represent the Environmental Protection Agency from Washington, D.C."

Erric's ears deafen to the words and he dreams with his eyes open for the rest of the presentation. His inner voice blurts out, God, she's still so gorgeous! Startled, Erric looks around, thinking someone might have heard him. He breathes a sigh of relief to find everyone has glued their attention on Katherine and are unaware of his love-sick stupor.

"So, I've detailed our positive intent behind this regulation and leave it to you to respond," Katherine finishes.

A murmured hubbub ensues until Stillwell gets the crowd's attention. "I think we otta get on paper something to say about each of these points and send that letter from us all to Washington… otherwise we'll be here all night and not git much done. Do I hear a motion to write a letter?"

"I'll make that motion," Erric asserts.

"I'll second that motion," Javier Jeminez shouts from the back. Heads spin and mixed emotions pass through the assembly of faces.

"Call the vote," Catbait announces. Distracted from Javier, the crowd quizzes over the fact that Catbait's usually soft voice rises to the rafters and fills the room with calm resolve.

Rod takes advantage of the momentum, "All those for it?"

In reply, the crowd yells in unity, "Aye!"

"Those against?" No one hears anything except water lapping sounds from beneath the floorboards.

Lacking a hammer and gavel, Rod smacks his hands together making the judgement a done deal, "Passed. Okay, the last item." Stillwell carefully surveys the room to make sure he has everyone's attention. "We all know 'bout the Bahamas taking John's traps and what happened to him. Nothing 'bout it's pretty. I hate to say this but don't think we can do nothing about it either."

The attendees erupt into a shouting rabble. Rod attempts to call them to silence. The crowd quiets until Jack takes advantage of this eye in the storm, "Let's organize a flotilla to rescue the traps!" Pandemonium breaks loose; the hurricane resumes at a full force five.

During the ruckus, Jack throws punches. It spreads like

a John Wayne western movie bar brawl.

Rod breaks up the main scuffle, which centers on Jack. Erric carefully assists while making no effort to hide his disgust at Jack's behavior. He realizes that Jack's mercurial moods rise and pass quickly and impetuously. Erric makes a sudden connection which brightens his assessment of his brother; Jack's like the apostle Peter who loves Christ but also acts impulsively.

Physical and verbal squabbles continue until Rod mounts the crude platform with a loose two by four and methodically whacks a support beam: whack… whack… whack.

Finally, the pandemonium stills. "I move to adjourn this meeting," Rod evenly but firmly declares. Angry but resigned, voices choked with emotion rapidly respond.

"Second."

"Vote."

Stillwell calls out, "All for?"

Half-hearted voices respond, "Aye."

Not waiting for nays, Rod announces, "Meetin' adjourned." But as he raises his hands to clap a final pronouncement, he pauses in mid-air. "First, could we all bow our heads and remember our good friend, John Thorman."

The men all grimly close their eyes and assume the

stance of prayer. A scant few bow their heads and become aware of their own breathing and heartbeat while they earnestly pray.

A few moments later Rod breaks the solemn silence, “Lord, I thank you for makin’ John my friend… well, everybody’s friend. Bless his wife and family in this hard time. Amen.” He resolutely claps his hands together signaling both a definite “amen” and the end of the meeting.

The crowd quietly converses and mingles among themselves.

If Javier Gonzales was wearing a hat, it would be in his hands as he quietly approaches Erric. “If there’s anyting we can do, let us know. Por favor?”

Somewhat taken aback Erric makes solid eye contact in silence, giving his answer heartfelt weight. “Yes. I will. I really needed to hear that. Thanks, Javier.”

Gonzales departs, and Fred Hammond takes his place. “Erric Thorman. I’m Fred Hammond… reporter for channel 4.”

Erric manages a smile as he mimics Fred’s on air sign off, “This… is Fred Hammond.”

“Yeah, this… is me.” They chuckle together. “Hey, I’d like to talk to you on film about the lobster trap situation. Say early tomorrow?”

Erric latches upon the opportunity to shine a spotlight on his plight, “Yeah. Yeah, good idea. How about my place? 7:30?”

“Done. Randy and I will be there.”

Erric approaches Katherine who’s been patiently waiting at a discreet distance.

“Hello, stranger.” Erric hears a slight tremor in his voice.

“Hello, yourself,” she responds carefully. “Sorry about your father.” There’s a short yet painful pause while Erric looks elsewhere and turns back to her.

“How about a walk along the docks?” Erric manages.

“That’s a good idea,” Katherine finishes.

<•{{{><

They stroll in silence, taking in the sights and smells on the pier, not daring to acknowledge their stolen glances at each other.

“I’ve really missed you,” Erric finally admits.

“I missed you, too, Erric.”

Erric’s head is swimming in deep water. He has to cut to the chase… he sees no other way. “So, where did you go and why?”

"Direct and to the point. That's the Erric I know, and I'm glad that hasn't changed."

"I'm just tryin' to let you know what's going on in my head, but I can't seem to make much sense of it anyway," Erric struggles.

"You're not alone, Ricky."

Erric's heart warms at her pet nickname for him. He hopes to return the feeling, "It's good to be with you even for just a few minutes, Kath."

Katherine smiles warmly at him, walks a few steps forming her next words and stops to face him. "We have a lot of ground to cover. I don't think one night will do it. Besides, I have a phone call to make."

Erric takes this in, sighs, and resigns with a compromised smile, "I guess that's good night. Until next time?"

Katherine smiles with her lips in a subtle quirky twist, "I guess that's good night, Captain Trap." They chortle under their breaths.

Although they unconsciously incline their bodies toward each other a pregnant pause underlines their reluctance to touch. Erric answers, "Yes, good night, missy."

Katherine continues to smile as she turns and glides into the night.

CHAPTER 5:

Surprise Voyage

The eastern sky has brightened to reveal three silhouetted men emerging out of hiding to converse in low tones. They survey the docks to see if anyone is looking as they stalk to the *Sonny Bays*.

The boat heads into the rising sun revealing the men checking their AR-15 rifles.

<•{{{><

Erric awakens and looks out his window searching for the *Sonny Bays* only to see an empty slip. "Holy hades! Where's the boat?" Erric shouts out.

"Watch your language, son," Mamie yells from her bed and grabs her abdomen in pain.

Erric hears banging at the door. "What's goin' on?" Rod Stillwell yells with Catbait at his side. "Where's the *Bays*?"

Erric lets Stillwell in and answers, "I don't know." He sees the empty couch, "Jack's missing, too. What's that fool up to now?"

Rod attempts to calm Erric, "Let's don't jump ta any conclusions. How 'bout usin' the radio?"

Mamie enters while tying her robe sash. Erric glances around at the back of the radio to make sure the tubes are glowing. He catches Mamie's eye. She tightens her lips and then exits to the bedroom saying, "I'll be prayin'."

Erric "This is base to the *Sonny Bays*, over." Erric unconsciously rocks back and forth impatiently. He tries two more times to get a response.

"This is *Sonny Bays* to base, over," Jack laconically replies.

"Jack, where…" Erric looks back toward Mamie's bedroom and lowers his voice. "Where in Hades are you? Over."

"In the Gulf Stream, over."

"Curses," Erric whispers. "What are you doin'?"

"Getting our traps back."

Rod Stillwell draws in a big breath and slowly lets it out while shaking his head. He locks eyes with Erric, who keys the radio. "Jack, please. Turn around and come back."

"I'll be home when the job's finished," Jack announces resolutely.

Rod holds out his hand, and Erric passes the radio handset to him. "Hey, Jack. This's Rod. Be reasonable. Don't tangle wi' tuh Bahamian Coast Guard."

"*Sonny Bays* to base," Jack formally announces. "Out."

A polite knock reveals Fred Hammond and Randy Born at the door with Catbait. "Yeah, come on in," Erric tells them.

"I think we should call tuh Coast Guard," Rod solemnly states.

"I tink so too, Mon," Catbait nods in agreement.

"Could you do it? I'm too worked up," Erric hands over the microphone to Rod.

Erric turns to the newsmen, "Got a lot going on. My kid brother has hijacked the boat. He thinks he's gonna try to nab our traps from the Bahamians."

"This is Rod Hammond from Stillwell Fisheries on the Thorman's radio to U.S. Coast Guard Cutter Intrepid, over," Rod announces.

"I take it you're not on board with this caper?" Fred Hammond quietly asks Erric.

"No way… well, I don't trust him to do it right."

Hammond carefully and quietly responds, "You know, having eyes on your boat makes everybody behave," and points to the film camera Randy carries at his side.

"This is Captain Pembroke on board the U.S. Coast Guard Cutter Intrepid, over."

"We got a situation," Rod radios back.

Mamie stares out her kitchen window at the empty dock and bare horizon. Rod Stillwell looks at her from sipping his coffee at the kitchen table, noticing her locks of hair spilling out of her bun to adorn her face. He interprets her flyaway hair as an indicator of her distressed mood. "Dear, Lord. Keep Jack safe out there," Mamie prays out loud to the expanse of saltwater.

"You know he's still just a kid. With a littl' dumb luck he'll pull through, God willin'," Rod assures Mamie.

Almost forgetting he was there, Catbait reminds them of his presence by bowing his head and praying out loud, "Lord, we put dis all in yer hands. Who are we to know your plans? Amen."

Mamie opens her brimming eyes, "Thanks, Sonny. Would you like more coffee?"

"Yes. I'll get it," Catbait gets up.

"Don't go spilling it, Catbait," Rod teases as Mamie forces a smile at the ongoing joke.

"I usually don't mean to. Yes, mon?" Catbait smiles.

"John always says he can count on Catbait coffee stains…" Mamie catches herself, "That's what John used to say."

Catbait miraculously pours coffee without incident and heads for the door. “I’m gonna make myself scarce.”

Rod & Mamie sit in silence. “I miss him a whole lot, too,” Rod sympathizes.

“It don’t seem real… that he’s gone,” Mamie whispers.

“I’m missin’ em like he wuz my own brother,” Rod confesses. Mamie drops her gaze to the floor. Rod pauses then reassures her, “Mamie, you know I’m just next door.”

“Thanks.”

CHAPTER 6:
Delicate Reunion

Against the fiery ball of the sun, a pelican swoops into the glistening reflection of the sun off the ocean to catch a fish. The pelican rises to sit on the surface. It tosses its head back in quick jerks to align the fish's head down its throat, then swallows with contentment.

Katherine smiles at the memories triggered by the pelican's breakfast ritual. She rocks slowly in her father's chair on the porch of the Stillwell home. Erric sits on the steps by her side. "So, I guess we just wait…" Erric says with resignation.

"Sometimes we don't have much choice," she replies.

Erric studies her as she gazes into the distance and is surprised to notice a detail which had previously escaped him, "You're still wearing the crucifix I gave you."

"I've never taken it off."

Confused, Erric's eyes dart around searching for answers. He tentatively ventures, "Kath, why did you leave?"

Katherine resolutely sits up straight and sets her chin, "It was better for everybody."

Erric chews on this but is not satisfied, "Wasn't better

for me, Kath."

"Ricky, you have no idea."

"Kath, try me."

"There are certain things a young girl should be ashamed of."

"What could you be ashamed of, Kath?"

Katherine closes her eyes and raises her face to the sun in an effort to let the warmth on her cheeks instill calmness, "I wish certain things had not happened."

Mystified, Erric stumbles out another question, "Such as?"

Katherine takes a long breath, then sighs, "Even a good thing can have bad consequences."

Erric gently persists, "Please… give me a clue, Kath."

"A new life can upset everything."

"But people start new lives all the time and end up happy."

"I'm talking about a new life in the form of a baby, Ricky."

"Huh?"

Katherine levels her eyes at Erric and spells it out, "Erric, I got pregnant."

A shocked Erric reacts, “Jeez. Uh… I’m sorry…Who did that to you?”

By now Katherine’s face goes slack. She breaks into tears, sobs and responds,

“It’s complicated.”

Feeling helpless, Erric clams up. A woman in tears can be a deep mystery… and him not having a clue is downright dangerous. He figures no words are the right words in this situation. He retreats into his own thoughts. *Who did this to her? Some landlubber city guy? Did he rape her? I’ll kill the S.O.B.!*

Catbait seems to appear from nowhere, “Pembroke’s got Jack, mon.”

<•{{{><

A fuming Errick waits on the Coast Guard Station pier. The Intrepid finally slides into its slip and ties up. Captain Pembroke strides down the plank well ahead of two sailors who flank Jack.

“I’m too furious to even speak to your brother,” Pembroke bellows.

Erric stands his ground. The detail accompanying Jack catches up to Pembroke who commands them, “That will be all. Dismissed.”

Erric shoots eye daggers at Jack, who hangs his head to

hide.

"What kind of moron thinks he can take on the Bahamian Coast Guard's .50 Caliber machine guns with a couple of pea shooters? What's he doing with those things, anyway?"

Erric shakes his head, "Got me."

"This could have been an international incident." Pembroke grabs Erric's shoulder, "I've got Bahamian friends in uniform and your brother on the other… I want no part of being in the middle."

Erric fights for his composure, reminding himself that Pembroke's ranting at Jack.

"I could impound the *Sonny Bays*, but I know you need to eat. Now go before I change my mind. Dismissed."

<•{{{><

Erric drives stone-faced along US 1 while a silent Jack stares out the passenger window. Jack's expression brightens. "I got an idea. We could make a lot of money and buy more traps, man."

"What the heck are you talking about, Jack?"

Jack directs an all-knowing smile at his brother. "It would just be catching a few square groupers."

Erric shoots him a puzzled glance, "Square grouper?"

Jack clarifies, “You know… bales of grass.”

Erric whips his head in Jack’s direction, “Pot?” Jacks nods his head nonchalantly.

Erric pulls the car over in the middle of the Vaca Cut bridge. “Get out,” he commands Jack. They both exit the car and meet at the guardrail overlooking the swiftly moving water driven by tide change. In a surprise maneuver, Erric throws Jack over the railing and into the water fifteen feet below. Jack finally breaks the surface, sputtering. The swift current carries him away far from the bridge.

Erric yells down to him, “No square grouper. Ever!”

Jack pitifully whines from the distance, “But I’m only tryin’ to help!”

<•{{{><

In the lull between breakfast and lunch at Goodsprings Bar and Grill, Jazzie surveys the few lingering guests and determines that everyone seems happy. She nods to herself and pushes through the double swinging doors into the kitchen to find the dishwashers catching up from the breakfast rush.

“You boys ‘r doin’ good.” Jazzie complements the two newly hired teens toiling in the kitchen. “Keep up the hard work,” she purrs over her shoulder as she retreats into to the dining room. The teens study her figure, swaying seductively as she walks away.

"She's hot," exclaims the surfer type with sun-bleached hair exclaims.

"Yeah, maybe she'll give us benefits if we please her," suggests his dark-haired buddy. They mischievously smile at each other.

Outside the kitchen door, Jazzie surveys the bar and watches Erric interact with a fellow lobsterman. When their conversation ends, she moves in. "You doing okay here, Erric? Another beer?" Erric shrugs.

The bar front door opens to reveal a soggy Jack who spots Erric and Jazzie. Jack humbles himself before his brother. "I had time to think, and the water woke me up. I hear ya loud and clear. We good, man?"

Erric looks Jack up and down, "I think you're all wet."

Jack's face falls. Erric bursts out in laughter, "I had ya, didn't I?"

Visibly relieved Jack catches on that Erric is teasing, "Thanks, for that… I think." Erric continues laughing while Jack's chagrin fades.

"Jazzie, a beer for Jack, please." When he sits down, Jack leaves a seat in between him and Erric.

"So, let's talk seriously about makin' some money, Jack. Legal money. Not just for traps, but also for mom's fibrosis operation." They both reflect for a moment.

A few sips later Jack pipes up, “In my travels I got hold of some Columbian…” Erric scowls. “… coffee.” Erric chuckles. Jack continues, “It’s the best coffee you ever tasted. Especially made with a French press.”

“Coffee’s coffee. What’s the big deal?”

Jack argues, “You have to taste it to understand.”

Erric frowns, “So how does it make us money?”

“We make runs to Columbia, sell it here with a good markup.”

“Who do we sell it to?”

“We could sell it to Catbait but he’d probably spill it.” Jack continues as Erric chuckles, “We sell it to anybody who likes excellent coffee. We could even open up a shop and sell it as premium coffee for triple the price.”

“I don’t think there’s a market for expensive coffee…” Erric objects.

“Anybody want to talk beer?” Jazzie offers as she leans on the counter close to Erric. Jack pretends to be interested in something outside the window.

Javier and a couple of buddies approach the bar, but Jazzie stops them in their tracks. “What are you guys doing here?”

Slightly taken aback Javier replies, “We’re here to drink

beer."

"You'll have to drink a whole lot to make up for the business I'm losin'." Her words perplex Javier. She continues her outrage, "You Cubans cut into the local catch... less lobster, less money for locals, less beer I sell. Got it?"

From across the room Deputy Sheriff Larry Beeker hears the tone in Jazzie's voice. Trying to appear casual he draws closer and sidles into the conversation. "You okay, Jazzie?" He smiles at Javier and company.

"I'm fine!" Jazzy wants nothing to do with his attempts to placate her and stomps away.

Jazzy bursts into the kitchen, startling the small staff. "Island beaners!" She turns her glare at the two teens washing dishes and frying potatoes. "Somebody needs to do somethin' to run 'em off!"

Out in the dining area Beeker quips, "Our little gardenia. Easily bruised." Jack's puzzled so Beeker volunteers an explanation, "Some lobstermen don't like the Cubans abandoning the crowded waters of Miami and moving down here. The Cubans compete for the same scarce lobsters as the locals."

CHAPTER 7:
Clearing the Decks

Katherine closes her eyes to enjoy the sensation of the warm morning sun on her delicate face tempered by a cool ocean breeze. She's in her new favorite place, the porch rocking chair.

"Mornin', Kath," Erric greets Katherine as he approaches her. "I thought you'd be gone by now."

"I decide to take a few days off to think," she answers without making eye contact.

"Whatcha thinkin'?" Erric asks.

"My next step."

"What are the choices?"

"Don't know yet."

Erric turns to scan the horizon for what seems to hold Katherine's attention. He swivels to study her face and realizes it's her thousand-yard stare at nothing. He'll try anything to snap her out of it, "Hey, let's have some fun, Kath. Like we used to."

"Like what?"

"How about a good ol' fashioned date?"

Katherine turns to him and quietly smiles.

Erric turns on the charm, “I’ll pick you up here this afternoon after lunch.”

“It’s a date,” she flatly responds.

Erric wanders off and feels vaguely unsettled. He needs wisdom to deal with this.

<•{{{><

“Catbait.” Erric calls out at the door of the processing room of Stillwell Fisheries. No answer. He ventures further into the room.

Jack enters the doorway, “Erric.”

“Yeah,” a slightly irritated Erric answers.

“Gotta talk to you.”

“What about?”

“I need to apologize,” Jack blurts out.

Erric struggles with his instinct to lash out, “I’m listening.”

“I’m a goof up, man,” Jack admits.

“That’s for sure. What else is new?”

“I’m sorry.”

“That’s the truth. You’re a sorry excuse for a human,”

Erric sneers.

Jack cautiously moves close, “Yeah, and I look up to you. I want you to be my brother again.”

“Seriously?” Erric mocks him.

“Serious as a heart attack.”

“There’s no way you can straighten out the garbage you’ve dumped on me and the family,” Erric challenges.

Jack bursts at the seams, “I’m sorry!”

Erric mocks him, “Fishsticks!”

Erric just pulled Jack’s trigger. The younger brother charges and lands three quick soft punches into Erric’s chest as he shouts, “I. LOVE. YOU!”

Erric instinctively returns a solid hook to Jack’s mouth, busting his lip, then registers surprise, “What did you say?”

Gasping for breath and through bloody lips, Jack repeats softly, “I love you.” He adds softly, “You’re my brother, man.”

Erric’s mixed emotions whirl at hurricane force while he staggers in place, attempting to comprehend. It dawns on him, “Yeah. Yeah. All right.”

This relieves Jack, “Good. Thanks.” Their eyes go elsewhere in thought, then find each other again. Simultaneously nodding heads, they grin broadly, laugh and bear hug each other.

<•{{{><

Erric knocks on the door of the Stillwell house. Katherine answers in an old tie dye T-shirt and cutoff jean shorts. She instantly senses Erric's unrest. "Are you okay, Ricky?"

He looks away momentarily, "Yeah. Just had a serious discussion with my brother." He swings around as if he hasn't seen her before, "You look great, Kath."

"Thanks, Ricky. What now?"

"Saddle up."

Erric opens the front passenger door to the dark turquoise blue 1964 Chevy Impala with white rag top. His dad scored it off a friend whose wife died. Katherine graciously smiles to acknowledge Erric's gallant deed and glides into the seat. He closes her door and walks around to enter the driver's side. Once behind the wheel he announces, "This isn't right."

Katherine's smile broadens as Erric exits and walks around to open her door. "Move over," he gently tells her and sits next to her.

Erric continues smiling as he gets out and walks around to the driver's side. Sliding behind the wheel and now sitting hip to hip with Katherine, he declares, "That's better!"

They bust out in peals of laughter. Katherine giggles

as she asks Erric, "Do you still pull that routine on all your dates?"

"Only the ones with you," He teases.

They traverse the gravel road to the highway. Erric runs down the list of details he and his dad added to the car: half-moon chrome eyelids on the headlights; blue translucent plastic dots in the middle of each taillight, and chrome eyelids acting as rain shields at the top exterior of all four windows. It's his now, and even more precious since it used to be dad's car.

The large squarish boat-like Chevy sits in front of Goodsprings Bar & Grill.

Inside at the bar, Erric holds a nearly empty beer glass, the latest in a series. He's wearing a sly look while Katherine laughs, "Thank God, literally, that you haven't changed, Ricky."

"What did you expect? I'm still me."

Jazzie pushes off from her vantage point down the bar and busts in addressing Erric, "Hey, you're having too much fun over here." Still laughing, Erric turns to look at her and realizes she is barely smiling. His laugh fades and Jazzie realizes he's read her too well. Still ignoring Katherine, Jazzie offers, "More beer?"

Katherine breaks the brief silence, "So it's Jazzie now?"

“Yeah, to my friends,” Jazzie coldly retorts.

“Can we start over, Jean?” Katherine asks. Erric doesn’t like the way this is going.

Jazzie continues her attack, “How do you and I make up for lost time we never had in the first place, Katherine?”

“Kath, how about an ice cream soda?” Erric meekly suggests.

“Rick, you’ve been slugging beers like they’re going out of style. You sure you can drive?”

“Who’s countin?” Jazzie interjects under her breath.

Erric pretends he doesn’t hear Jazzie. “I’m a champion at Pong. I’ll bet I’m sober enough to beat you. If I win, I drive.”

Katherine smiles broadly, “You’re on!”

<•{{{><

The Chevy top is down and Katherine’s blond hair wisps in the breeze as she navigates the custom automobile down the Overseas Highway. Erric slumps happily in the passenger seat. They pull up at Anderson’s Drugs.

Erric swigs an extra-large shake as Katherine sips a smaller version from a straw. They laugh … and then laugh some more.

Erric punches the jukebox to play a Florida rock group

singing a silly but catchy song about a tiny black egg. Following like a non sequitur, a British soft rock hit about hiding love slows down their bodies; they fall into a waltz done swing style. Erric catches his breath as he rediscovers how magically Katherine responds to his lead, as if they are performing a rehearsed dance in a contest. Erric has never danced with a more graceful woman.

Minutes drift away without a care.

<•{{{><

Erric drives Katherine up to the Stillwell home, "I had fun. Let's stay on the wave. How 'bout a movie later?"

Katherine pauses, "I guess I'm game. What time is the movie?"

"After sundown," he teases.

<•{{{><

Erric and Katherine sip beers as they sit in an anchored boat within distant view of a drive-in movie which plays silently.

"So, what's this free movie about?"

Erric puts on a formal voice, "Only the best for my Missy. It's kind of horror film about a big shark."

"Is it as scary as the one about the little demon girl whose head spins around?"

Erric mumbles, “I dunno. Let’s see.”

“Huh, look at that. Swimming alone at night’s dumb,” Katherine comments.

“Naw, it’s usually fine,” Erric protests.

The on-screen swimmer thrashes as an unseen force pulls her under. Erric chuckles, “Well, there you go. Guess you’re right.”

Katherine watches Erric’s profile in the screen’s glow; her mind far away. “Rick. I guess I should just come out and say it. Deal with the fallout.”

“What’s that, Missy?”

“It’s you.”

“What’s me, Kath?”

“You’re the father.”

This confuses Erric, “But what about that guy somewhere… wherever you’ve been all this time?”

“It’s all too complicated. I didn’t want to screw up your life. You had a scholarship… bright future. I didn’t want everyone to know about what we’d been doing.”

“Yeah, that would’ve been a little difficult…”

“I was lonely. The winters in D.C. where I lived with aunt Linda were so cold. I watched snowflakes dancing around the streetlights at night. It reminded me of fish schooling on the reefs here. I missed the warm, clear water. The tropical sun. I was so homesick."

Erric attention raptly focuses on her beautiful face.

"I missed you most, Ricky."

"Good Lord, Kath."

They move in for a kiss, but Katherine interrupts. "Please don't kill me, Ricky. I gotta pee… really bad."

Erric is both frustrated and tickled. Katherine maneuvers to the stern. "No peeking, Eric. This is not my best pose." Erric dutifully turns away and can't help but giggle. There's a splash. Erric whips around to find Katherine's gone.

"Kath! Kath!"

Katherine surfaces and pretends to struggle in the water. Without hesitation Erric dives overboard fully clothed. When he reaches her, Katherine laughs, "Gotcha!"

"Kath, you freaked me out."

"You thought I was being pulled down by a shark?"

"It's not funny," Erric tries to suppress a laugh.

They swim playfully in the moonlight and hold a kiss underwater until their aching lungs drive them to the surface.

<•{{{><

Erric pulls the boat up to the Stillwell dock and bids Katherine good night with a gentleman's kiss in case Mamie or Rod are watching. He shoves off and heads to the Thorman pier. A flickering across the small bay catches his eye. He throttles down to find the light gathering strength. It's a fire.

Erric guns the motor. As he covers the distance to the far shore, the flames engulf a stack of lobster traps. Against the tall leaping inferno, he spots two silhouetted figures fleeing the scene.

The boat bow crunches the shore, and he leaps out, but it's too late to douse the fire. The fire has destroyed the traps. In a cursory investigation, he finds a matchbook from Goodsprings Bar.

Deputy Beeker's cruiser shows up, "Hey, is that you, Erric?"

"Yup, It's me, Yeti."

"Your mom called in. Just happened to be nearby. You see anything?"

"Looked like two guys, I think. Weren't big guys. I found this."

Beeker takes the matchbook. "This might help, thanks."

"These your traps?" Larry asks sensitively.

"No, I think it might be Javier's."

Beeker's face draws tight, "Mercy. Have mercy, Lord…"

CHAPTER 8:
Charting a Course

Erric's gaze wanders off the road and out his car window up to a large pelican flying point position in a "V" formation of eight birds traveling downwind. They nearly match his speed of 45 mph. He guesses the enormous bird may be an older male judging by his size and the large droopy pouch under his bill. It's amazing to see this prehistoric looking foul gracefully choreograph the group by alternately flapping his wings and then resting the group in well-timed glides.

Erric lowers his attention to the road, spots Larry Beeker's patrol car on Grassy Key and pulls over. Larry Beeker's uniformed back juts out from the top of mangroves growing along the shoreline. Erric rounds the corner of a clump of vegetation to discover a private moment between Beeker and Jazzie.

Jazzie lies on a towel near the water, dressed only in the barest of bikinis and a pair of sunglasses. Larry plucks white petals from a gardenia and drops them one by one on her abdomen. The last petal floats down to her torso and seems to wait for an answer. Jazzie brushes the flower fragments away like they are annoying insects and turns her face away from Larry.

Eric decides he's seen too much already and quietly retreats to his car.

"Hey, Erric," Larry calls out. "Just the man I want to see."

"Yeah? I saw your car and wanted to know what's going on."

Larry smiles broadly, "Solved the burning traps case. Jazzie's dishwashers caved and confessed. They claim she told them to do it, but Jazzie denies it. You know how sexy Jazzie can act. I think their hormones got the best of them."

"So, what's gonna happen?"

"The kids will go to juvie. I told them to never show their faces around here if they know what's good for 'em. The boys have no money for restitution. Javier's out of luck."

"Erric drops his eyes, "Tough break for Jav. Sounds like it's wrapped up."

Larry cocks his head, "For me, it is. We may call you as a witness. And Jazzie's ticked off she has to find two dishwashers to replace them. Somehow, she thinks you owe her since you're the sole witness. You know how hard it is hard to find young people to work."

Erric agrees as he nods, "Yup, Keys Fever. Kids split for the mainland the morning after graduation."

<•{{{><

Catbait drags a broken trap into the cool shade of Stillwell Fisheries processing room. Rod Stillwell looks up to acknowledge him and returns to finishing repair work on another.

“I hope Javier appreciates this,” Rod wonders out loud.

“A gift well-received is a blessing to the giver. Ya, mon?” Catbait answers.

Rod chuckles at Catbait’s simple wisdom, “Yeah, that’s the way the good Lord designed us.”

Eric darkens the door, smiling broadly, “Are you all finished?”

Rod smiles from the side of his mouth as Catbait delivers a short cackle.

Catbait teases Erric, “You sleep late. Yah, mon?”

“It took me a while to do my usual two hundred one armed pushups,” Erric stretches and flexes his arms. They all share smiles.

“Ran into Beeker. The two kids at Goodsprings burned the traps. They’re going to juvie.”

“Well, these traps should more or less settle this whole thing,” Rod asserts.

Outside, a Lincoln Continental pulls up. The prominent chrome grill reminds Erric of the recent movie about a black cocaine dealer. Rod exits to greet the driver in a black suit and tie while Erric saunters to the door to watch. He catches a few words and realizes this is the loan officer from Rod's bank who is presenting Rod with a folder of paper.

Erric catches one of the suit's words, "foreclosure." He thinks to himself the car is fitting for a banker. There's not much difference between pedaling cocaine and loaning money.

The banker pulls away and Rod reenters the room. His mood is dark. Erric and Catbait get busy fixing traps, trying to ignore what could get explosive.

"Daddy," Katherine calls out half-way between the fishery and the house.

"Yes, Katherine?"

"Please come to the house. I need to speak to you," Katherine implores.

A still fuming Rod walks with heavy steps out of the room and toward the house.

"Rod's acting like a pressure cooker about to explode," Erric comments to Catbait.

"Is it not understandable, mon?"

"Yeah. Sometimes he's a little scary… and mysterious," Erric admits. Catbait sagely nods in agreement.

"You know something else that's mysterious and scary, Catbait?" Catbait stops working to give Erric his full attention. "Women."

The wise old Bahamian smiles sagely, "Every man asks that question, no?"

"So, what's the answer?"

With a twinkle in his eye and his smile growing ever wider, Catbait stares unblinking and slowly shakes his head "no" until Erric busts out laughing. Catbait joins in. They are unaware of Rod walking quickly and determinedly into the fish house.

Trailing Rod to the door Katherine yells, "Daddy, no!"

Erric stands like a deer in the headlights as Rod closes the last couple of steps in almost a single leap while cocking back his arm. He lands a solid, powerful punch to Erric's solar plexus. Erric pitches backwards as he doubles over in pain, landing on and demolishing a broken trap on the floor.

Helpless, Katherine looks away, then back again. She is afraid to interfere.

With barely contained anger Rod points his finger at Erric, "You owe me my daughter's life!" Stillwell strides out with finality, ignoring everyone.

"Sorry, Ricky," Katherine whispers.

Still doubled over on the ground with the wind knocked out of him, Erric struggles but manages a breathy squeak, "It's okay, Kath. He's right."

<•{{{><

The aroma of boiling celery, bay leaves, black pepper, allspice and a key lime slices waft from a large pot in a corner of the processing room. Erric quietly watches Catbait stir the brew.

Catbait breaks the silence, "You feel better, mon?"

"Yeah. I'm a little sore, but still upset. Lot's going on."

"It all come out good, ya mon? Ready for lobster?"

Erric nods his head as Catbait pulls a lobster off ice. He holds the crustacean as a child would hold an airplane and does a little twirl on his feet like a youngster dancing. He puts the lobster through some barrel rolls, changes it deftly between his hands before suddenly plunging it headfirst into the roiling water.

"You got to keep 'em guessing. Be sneaky, ya mon? You know Goombay Summer?"

"Heard of it. Never been," Erric nods.

Catbait pulls two beers out of the fridge and the men pop them open, raise them for a quick toast. He winks, "To

Goombay Summer and those who sleep late next morning, yah mon?"

Erric's thoughts ferment a moment until his face brightens with an idea.

The sound of a vehicle pulling up brings Erric back to the moment. Javier and his entire family drive up in a worn early model Ford pickup truck. Erric exits the building to greet them, "Welcome!" he jubilantly exclaims.

"Buenos dias, senior," Javier beams back and includes Catbait who appears at the door. He points to each of his family "This is my wife, Maria holding our new la Bébé, Nina." He turns to the truck bed, "This my son, Ernesto, and his young brother, Pepito."

"We got some traps for ya," Erric smiles. "Let's get 'em loaded."

Erric and Catbait help Javier and sons quickly stack the repaired traps in the truck like it's a joyful game.

The family climbs back into the truck as Erric warmly smiles at Maria in the front seat holding her precious newborn. Maria openly beams back as a proud mother. The classic image of maternal love noticeably touches Erric.

"Please thank Senior Rod for this, por favor?" Javier says through the truck window.

"Will do. Audios, amigo," Erric says. As their truck

chugs off down the pebble road, he breathes deeply; grateful that he has a good feeling in his gut for a change.

CHAPTER 9:
Covert Passage

Erric awakes in the gathering dawn, aware of a strange sound. Out his window he discerns the shape of what is probably Catbait with his arms raised, facing the sea and talking to himself. Erric strains to listen but cannot make out the words. Catbait transitions into singing in an unintelligible language. Erric remains transfixed for a few minutes… mystified.

<•{{{><

The sun rises over the horizon of the Atlantic Ocean on the far side of Conch Key. Without benefit of direct sunlight, Erric takes advantage of the brightening sky to load the *Sonny Bays*. Katherine arrives and puts two and two together. "You're not going out to stand off the Bahamian Coast Guard, are ya?"

"Got any other ideas?"

"Rick, that's dangerous and you could get arrested!"

"Kath, I gotta do it. No choice."

"I'll call Bob Pembroke and get you stopped."

Erric notes Kath calls Captain Robert Pembroke, "Bob." He sneers but it surprises him; he feels a tinge of jealousy.

"Don't go or I'll call the Coast Guard, Rick!"

"Kath, you'll only make things worse. Pembroke won't get our traps back."

Frustrated, Katherine plays the only card she has left, "If you're so set on this, then I'm coming along to keep you out of trouble."

Erric freezes. His body language gives away stages of inner turmoil: shock, disgust, and then he relaxes into what appears to be resignation. "Okay, if you're going along let's get more safety gear."

"Good idea," she agrees.

"Let's take some signal flares," he suggests.

Katherine leads Erric to the storage locker in the fish house, opens the door and peers into the cramped aisles between shelves crammed with marine supplies. "He used to have some, Ricky. Kept them near the door. Where are they now?"

"I think he moved them into the far corner," Erric offers.

Katherine moves deeper into the storage area while Erric quietly opens a refrigerator and takes out a pack of flares. He backs out through the shed door and slams it shut.

Katherine screams, "Rick!"

Through the door, Erric raises his voice so she can hear him, "Sorry. Can't risk you gettin' hurt."

Erric locks it just before Katherine's body slams it while she screams, "But I can take care of myself!"

"By the way, your dad keeps the flares in the fridge now. Thinks it's safer."

"Shoot, Erric!" She chews her lip, while fingering the crucifix on her necklace. Her tone softens, "Erric, please listen to me."

Erric hears her emotional appeal and returns to listen at the door.

"Erric, look down." Her crucifix and chain appear from the crack under the door. "Erric, please put it on and don't take it off. I treasure it because you gave it to me. I want you to bring it back."

Erric picks up the crucifix, gazing at the fine details in the silver. He can see the suffering on Christ's face. Erric forces himself to shake the wave of emotions flooding over him. He croaks out, "Will do," and walks away.

Katherine bangs on the door, "Ricky. Ricky. Don't die like your father!"

Erric walks to the *Sonny Bays*, checking to see if Katherine's muffled cries have alerted anyone. He freezes at the sound of an automatic rifle cocking. A dark silhouette stands in the boat. "Jack's taken good care of it," Rod says matter-of-factly, looking up from studying the Colt AR-15 rifle in his hands.

Erric stands on the dock, hesitant to board the boat. Unfazed, Rod calmly addresses Erric again, "So, you locked her in storage."

Erric avoids sounding defensive, "Tryin' to keep her out of trouble."

"That's a switch," Rod says with a strange note of sarcastic approval.

Erric can't read Rod's face but boards the boat anyway and plops the flares down on top of a pile of gear. "Hey, I'll put these on my tab," he assures Rod.

Rod shifts position a couple of steps and turns on a working light. He watches Erric stowing supplies.

"That's Katherine's crucifix," Rod says with a tinge of surprise. Erric straightens and faces him while touching the necklace.

"It's a loan. She'll get it back."

Rod looks away, taking a moment to gather his thoughts. He turns to Erric while raising the AR-15 to hold it across his chest with both hands. "You're not takin' this." Without taking his eyes off Erric, he casually tosses the weapon overboard.

Erric suppresses his reflex to dive in after it but stares down Rod. It's a Mexican stand-off. Rod breaks the tense moment, "Put it on my tab."

Erric breaks into a nearly imperceptible smile.

Rod returns with a sly smile, "I'm going with you."

Erric tenses, "It's not your battle."

Rod forces a laugh, "I practically own the traps and this boat, too."

"He was my father."

"Your father is my best friend!" Rod realizes he used the wrong tense. "Was." He drops his voice, "Loved him like a brother."

Rod's words and his broken tone visibly moves Erric. After a moment passes, Erric gently asserts himself, "It'll be my trip."

Rod considers this and agrees, "Okay."

Erric is slightly surprised, but negotiations are not over. With quiet authority earned by a record of demonstrable wisdom, Rod affirms the ultimate point of agreement, "No guns." Rod grins wryly, "None… whatsoever."

Erric sighs, "Okay. Okay!" He bends down and removes a 9mm from his ankle holster.

Jack walks up to the boat and reacts to the empty canvas rifle bag at his feet on the dock, "Where is it?"

Erric looks at Rod but gets no help. He turns to Jack, "No guns this time" and he tosses his 9mm into the drink. A shocked Jack watches the ripples from the splash radiate across the tiny harbor. This resolute gesture from his brother coupled with the guilt of his recent foolish voyage seals the deal between the three men.

Jack jumps on board.

Mamie tootles along the dock, "Did ya get the bag of food I made?"

"Yes, mom. Thanks," Erric answers.

Mamie reacts to a distant sound then turns to Rod, "Here come the TV people …"

Rod quickly heads off Mamie's next sentence, "Yeah, I got my teeth in. Thanks, Mamie."

The WTVJ-News 4 sedan rolls up and Fred and Randy pile out. "We brought some insurance," Fred Hammond says to Rod as he points to the 16mm Frezzolini film camera Randy carries.

Asserting the captain's role, Erric answers him, "Thanks, Fred. We need all the help we can get." Hammond glances back at Rod, who ignores him and instead focuses his attention on Erric.

“We’ve got some more gear to bring aboard,” Fred announces. Erric acknowledges with a nod.

Catbait appears, “What we got here, mon?” The old salt points down the dock at an approaching group of half a dozen Cuban fishermen.

Fred Hammond cues Randy, who has already surreptitiously started filming.

“Buenos dias,” Javier called out.

“Good morning,” those on board call out a bit ragged with uncertainty.

“Senior Rod, thanks again for the traps,” Javier radiates.

“You’re very welcome, Jav.”

“Is there anything we can do, Senior Erric?”

“As a matter of fact,…” Erric stops, distracted by the Cubans turning their backs on him and opening up a path through them to reveal another gang of fishermen headed their way. The Cubans stand uneasily; not sure of what will happen.

The two factions eye each other warily as the shortest man elbows his way in front of the new arrivals. Darryl Collier ignores the Cubans and looks straight at Rod, “We’re here to help. Tells us what we can do.”

Rod looks at Erric who steps up to the plate again,

"Gentlemen…" He's again distracted… this time he sees Hammond look at Randy who twirls his finger to show he's still rolling.

"Mr. Hammond," Erric addresses with as much respectful authority he can muster, "Could we keep this off the record?" Fred shrugs and swipes his index finger across his neck at Randy, who nods and cuts his camera.

"All of you showing up today makes me proud to be a fellow fisherman in the Keys." Erric studies the crowd, finally resting his eyes on the TV crew. Not sure of whom to trust with his plan, Erric delivers a riddle to the crowd. "Yes, we need all your help. Listen carefully… lure the big fish in the morning. Lure the big fish in the morning."

Puzzled expressions dissolve into realization, prompting whispers.

Erric turns to his crew, "Okay, men. Let's cast off." Then he remembers and turns to the lobstermen on the dock, "Oh, and would somebody let Katherine out of the storeroom after we've cleared the harbor?"

Mamie waves to the boat far out in the small bay and frees Katherine. "Thanks, Mamie," Katherine says a little exasperated, then turns to sorrowfully to wave in sad silence at the disappearing boat.

Mamie touches her on the shoulder, "Come stay with me while the men are at sea."

<•{{{><

The nine-day-old waxing moon glows on the gently rippling mirrored water of Conch Key harbor. Inside the Thorman home Katherine finishes up a phone call, "I can't thank you enough, aunt Linda." She pauses for Linda's reaction and continues, "I would be there if I could. Please call me if his sniffles get worse." Katherine smiles, "Yes, I love you, too."

Katherine turns to Mamie, "Thank you for letting me make that long-distance call. I'll get some cash out of my purse…"

"Don't you dare. What are friends for?" Mamie assures her.

If someone were to watch through the window, they would see two women sharing their hearts deep into the night until they fall asleep on the coach, despite occasional static bursts from the marine radio.

CHAPTER 10:
Run the Gauntlet

The crescent moon rules the heavens off the coast of Andros Island, Bahamas. On board *Sonny Bays* Erric, Jack, Rod, and Catbait furiously pull lines of traps in the dimness of a working light. They empty each trap of lobster, clean it, and instead of returning them to the water, stack them high on the deck.

With the arduous task finally done, Rod relaxes on deck and sends up a prayer thanking God for providing this way of making a living. Just a hundred years ago lobster was worth next to nothing. Farmers used these shellfish for fertilizer and otherwise considered them as food for the poor. Now these appetizing creatures are more valuable than steak.

Fred Hammond scans the black horizon while Randy cradles his camera, waiting for daylight. Erric and Jack steal glances at each other. The heat of their animosity slowly cools.

Randy braces his camera on the side of the wheelhouse to capture a magnificent shot. The glowing sun seems to surface from the depths of the sea as a colony of gulls dive and dip into the water. Meanwhile, a pod of porpoises undulates over and under the surface.

An almost impossibly tall stack of lobster traps tower over the deck of the *Sonny Bays*. A bare semblance of lashing ropes does little to ensure their integrity.

The crew has worked all night to pull the traps and now rest while churning back toward Conch Key. Hammond scans the horizon from the bow while monitoring Randy, who films only carefully selected scenes to save film.

Erric saunters over to sit next to Jack on the deck. In silence, they spend a few minutes getting use to each other's presence.

Erric cuts the ice, "Hey, bro. That busted lip helps your general ugliness." Jack shoots him a look, but Erric's wry smile disarms him.

Jack fires one back, "You ought to get one. It might give you courage to call Shula back."

They both feel relief that this is going well.

Erric turns to Jack, "Hey… uh, look… I don't know if you want to, but could you tell me a little of what you've been doing all this time?"

"Some of it I don't want to even remember," Jack confesses. His eyes drift seaward, "I miss the Mamie. It was like seeing your own mother drown. Jim Reynolds, Yeti… I mean Beeker and I were fishing off the coast of Cuba and this monster of a storm pushed us onto the coastline in the dead of night."

Erric breaks in, “Beeker and Reynolds mention they were shipwrecked, but they refuse to talk about it.”

“I perfectly understand. Anyway, the Mamie busted up on a shallow reef just offshore and sank. Yeti and I barely made it ashore alive. They arrested us immediately.”

An alarmed Erric interrupts, “Arrested! What for?”

“Lucky us. We washed up at the site of a secret Russian missile base. The Cuban military and the KBG were on their usual patrol that night. They thought we were spies so threw us in prison.”

“Good Lord, Jack.”

“The worst part was that they threatened to execute us by firing squad at sunrise. That went on for three days. Waiting all night was torture… didn’t sleep much. On the third day we finally convinced them we weren’t spies and they set us free.”

Erric blows out a breath through his teeth, “I literally thank God you got out of that mess, bro.” He playfully punches Jack on his upper arm. A shaken Jack drops his head and smiles bitterly.

Erric takes a deep breath, “Well, we’re on an adventure here, too. To get home, we have to breeze past both the Bahamian and the U.S. Coast Guard.” Fist bump. Jack’s knuckles meet Erric’s. Their smiles broaden as they both hope for a re-bonding of their brotherhood.

<•{{{><

The marine radio in the Thorman house squawks to life. "Howsit rolling out there, Jimmy G? Over."

"Pretty smooth sailin'," Robin. Over."

Mamie stirs, "They're a little chatty out there."

Katherine clears her throat, "They sound like squawking gulls."

Coast Guard cutter *Intrepid* cruises toward the Gulf Stream on a perfect sunny day. Captain Pembroke stares at the coast guard radio puzzling over the inane communications among the usually tip lipped mariners.

"Have you seen the big fish?" chirps the radio.

"Not yet. You?"

"Naw. On the lookout, though."

"Breaker, breaker. This is Javier Hernandez, Captain of the *Ponce DeLeon* calling Coast Guard Cutter *Intrepid.* Over."

Pembroke picks up and keys the microphone, "This is Captain Pembroke of the Coast Guard Cutter *Intrepid.* Over."

"We need help. Our motor stopped. I tink we are about nine miles sout of Summerland Key. Over."

"Roger. We're out in the Gulf Stream south of you. Heading your way. Out." Pembroke commands the wheelhouse, "Bring us around for a new heading to their coordinates."

Mamie puts her coffee cup on the kitchen table and swivels from the radio to Katherine, "That's interesting. And a little strange."

Katherine shrugs and changes the subject, "So, I told you last night that I blamed Erric. It took a long time to shake that attitude. I'm convinced now that I love him. I even told him that. But I don't know how he feels."

Mamie nods in understanding, "Let's be like James Bond in the spirit. That means taking action right now. Let's pray." Katherine agrees with a nod, bows her head, and closes her eyes.

Mamie speaks boldly, "Dear Lord, you already know the outcome. We ask you to lead hearts in the right direction and pour Your love over these two people. Show Erric and Katherine the path you want them to follow. In Jesus's name, Amen."

Teary-eyed, Katherine agrees, "Amen."

Mamie's countenance shines, "God just gave me an idea. Let's rally the preacher and some prayer warriors and all pray at church."

Katherine lights up, "Yes. By all means."

Javier and his sons watch the horizon from their boat drifting dead in the water. They take turns using one set of binoculars. Little Pepito thinks he sees something. His older brother, Ernesto, takes the binoculars and double checks. He offers the binoculars to Javier, "Dad, it looks like the Coast Guard."

Javier refuses the binoculars, "That's okay. I trust your eyes," and strides to the wheel, starts the engine, and cranks up the radio.

"*Ponce de Leon* to *Intrepid*, over."

"Yes, *Ponce de Leon*, we are approaching to offer assistance. Over."

"Tank you, *Intrepid*. We just now start engine. It seem fine now. Over."

"Well, glad we might have been of help, *Ponce de Leon*. Out." Pembroke barks orders to the wheelhouse crew, "Reset our original course towards Andros Island."

The hot summer sun beats down on the white clapboard exterior of the church chapel. Katherine opens the front door for Mamie and turns to wave to an approaching Maria who nestles her baby Nina in her arms.

Katherine's sudden and urgent whisper in Mamie's ear startles her, "Mamie, Erric told all the other men they could help by solving a riddle: 'lure the big fish in the morning.'" Katherine pulls back to see Mamie's expression of agreement and continues, "So maybe the *Intrepid* is the big fish."

Mamie breaks into a soft, knowing smile and nods in agreement. They both turn and greet their friend in unison, "Buenos Dias, Senora."

Darryl Collier squints and smiles at the perfectly glorious day. He throttles down and cuts his engine. He and his mate check a chart. Ross grabs the radio and rasps out a message, "This is Captain Darryl Collier of the *Keys Queen* to Coast Guard cutter *Intrepid*. Over."

Pembroke smiles at the unmistakable voice, "This is the *Intrepid*, Darryl. Over."

"*Intrepid*, we are experiencing engine failure. Can you assist us? Over."

"What is your position, *Keys Queen*? Over."

"We are five nautical miles due south of Duck Key, Over."

"Noted *Keys Queen*. We are setting a course to you. Out."

<•{{{><

The *Sonny Bays* runs full speed on a westerly course plowing through the deep blue waters of the Gulf Stream for Conch Key. All eyes scan the horizon, especially behind them.

Jack approaches Erric at the wheel next to Catbait, "You don't think the Bahamians can catch us now, do you?"

Erric feigns a smile of confidence, "I'm counting on their coast guard to be hung over from Goombay Summer last night. That's why we timed the run for today."

"Brilliant. You came up with that?"

Erric turns to Catbait, who just smiles back. When he doesn't jump in, Erric continues, "Catbait gave me the idea… he didn't exactly spell it out."

<•{{{><

Mamie and Katherine sit on the front row of the chapel giving Pastor Kenyon their rapt attention as does the other dozen congregants. "We must trust God with everything, especially in dire straits like the Thormans have been going through," he intones. "Let us pray. Dear Lord, strengthen our faith…"

During the laboriously long prayer, the congregants one by one sneak out of the chapel to gather in the church kitchen. They huddle around a portable marine radio set to a discreetly low volume.

"… forgive us our trespasses as we forgive those who trespass against us…" Kenyon drones on.

One member sneaks in to tap Mamie and whisper in her

ear. Mamie hustles Katherine out of her seat. They are the last two to join the kitchen listening crew.

Under Erric's command the *Sonny Bays* continues to churn westward, the bow cutting and dividing each swell into two spewing plumes of white spray on either side.

He motions the crew to the wheelhouse. "Well, we're crossin' 'bout the middle of Gulf Stream. It's where dad wanted his ashes scattered. Anybody else think now's the time?" They silently acknowledge with a unanimous nod. Fred and Randy stand at a respectful distance.

Catbait speaks up, "Ya'll do it. I'll be at the wheel keeping us on course. And I'll be a' prayin', mon."

Erric, Jack and Rob congregate downwind at the starboard stern. Erric speaks up, "Anybody want to say anything?" The three stand in silence, aware of Catbait praying in tongues a few feet away.

Jack stares at the urn of ashes, "Dad, sorry I acted like an idiot and left like that. It surprised me you welcomed me home like you did, but when I think about it… that's you. You always loved first." He drops his gaze to the deck.

Rod drops his head, closes his eyes and prays, "Lord, I know I'll see John again although I'm not ready just yet. In the meantime, I'm going to miss the man who was like the brother I never had." Erric uncaps the clay vessel.

Randy wrestles between allowing this to be a private moment or intruding to capture it for posterity on film. Yes, I'm pursuing an ambitious career, but I must remind himself that life exists outside of the eyepiece of a camera; I have a soul. I'll film it and make that decision later. To keep a low profile, he slowly raises the camera to his shoulder and feels the familiar purring vibration through his hands and on his shoulder.

Erric looks to heaven, "We all love you, dad. I aim to live up to the standards you taught us… and let God rule."

Erric tips the jar, allowing the contents to sift down through the air to meld into the deep navy waters of the Florida Straits. Randy captures the three men huddled together, pans over and zooms into where the ashes meet the ocean. All stand in silence to commemorate the passing of a man's man of the sea.

One by one, the men return to the moment and resume scanning the horizon. Although very rusty in the spirit, Jack prays to himself, *Dear God, this is a mess. Please help us. Amen.*

Randy Born peers through his camera using the telephoto lens to survey the distance. He's puzzled about a speck in the sky. He yells out, "I think a plane's coming in from behind us!"

All eyes swing around to the stern and Fred Hammond abandons his lookout position at the bow.

The airplane drops its altitude to only a couple of hundred feet off the water and flies directly over the *Sonny Bays*. Randy exuberantly yells, "I got an excellent shot of it!"

The radio bursts with static over a distorted message. Erric throttles down to hear better.

"… spotter plane number one of Royal Bahamas Defence Force. Your vessel has lobster traps, which are the property of our government. We order you to turn around and return your cargo to Nassau Harbor. Over."

The tight group of coffee sipping listeners shoot alarmed looks at each other at the pilot's warning. They strain to hear while Mamie whispers in tongues. Pastor Kenyon quietly enters the kitchen unnoticed. "AMEN!" he powerfully projects. The group reflexively jumps in unison. He continues, "Turn that up so we can hear it." The group relaxes, a few parishioners smile nervously, and Mamie jumps up to bring Pastor Kenyon a cup of coffee.

On board the *Intrepid*, Captain Pembroke's facial lines deepen as he absorbs the Bahamian pilot's second radio warning. "This is the Royal Bahamas Defence Force. Your lobster traps are the property of our government. Identify yourself. Over."

"This is the *Albatross* calling Coast Guard cutter *Intrepid*. Over."

"This is the *Intrepid*. Go ahead, *Albatross*. Over."

"We're adrift. Out of gas. Over."

Pembroke nearly bursts an angry artery in his neck, then has an epiphany. He grabs the microphone, "Attention all boats. Attention all boats. The jig's up. Those calling for help just have to drift for a while. I've got bigger fish to fry. Out."

Barely able to contain himself, Pembroke commands the bridge to make a heading northeast toward the midpoint between Andros Island and Conch Key. He intensely monitors the radar screen.

Pembroke keys his radio, "This is U.S. Coast Guard Cutter *Intrepid*. I command the vessel being called by the Bahamian Defence Force to identify itself. Over."

Like a snake striking its prey, Erric grabs Catbait's wrist and forces him to throw his coffee onto the marine radio. The electronics sputter, crackle, and produce both steam and smoke. Erric shoves the throttle to full speed.

On the cutter, Pembroke pulls back from the loud burst of static.

Catbait is aghast while Erric slyly smiles at him. "Don't worry, I forgive you for knocking out the radio." Catbait catches on.

Jack pipes up from behind, "I'd call that plausible deniability."

On board the *Keys Queen*, Darryl Collier rasps over the radio, "Attention all lobstermen. Time to pull in the net." Up and down the Florida Keys commercial fishing vessels change course and push their engines to the max.

The Bahamian Coast Guard Plane dives at the *Sonny Bays* as if he is strafing them. The crew literally hit the deck in prone positions except Randy Born, who twists on his feet to photograph the passing plane.

"That guy's nuts!" yells Jack.

Erric shouts, "Can't guarantee he's sober either."

Fred Hammond goes into action, "Randy got any gaffer tape?" Hammond and Randy rip pieces of duct tape off a roll. They use the two-inch strips of light grey adhesive to spell out "WTVJ-4 TV" on the wheelhouse roof. The plane makes another pass while Randy holds up the camera while waving and pointing at it with his other hand.

"I don't see any guns on that thing," Rod assures.

"Could he be a kamikaze pilot, mon?" Catbait cackles.

"Another plane!" Fred Hammond shouts. All eyes follow Fred's gesture to see a single-engine aircraft bearing down on them from the Keys to the east. The newcomer pilot crowds the airspace forcing the Bahamian craft to retreat.

"Hey, is that Jim Reynolds up there?" Rod asks.

"Yeah, I think it's him," Erric confirms. He then jumps up and down on the deck shouting to the sky, "Hey, Jim! Welcome to the party." Jim makes a polite pass tipping his wings and waving through the cockpit window.

Catbait's voice brings more joy, "Loyal friends are a blessing from God, yes mon?"

"Jim's sure enough a great friend," Jack agrees.

<•{{{><

A grim Pembroke tightens his grip on the microphone, "This is Captain Robert Pembroke, captain of the U.S. Coast Guard Cutter *Intrepid* to the Royal Bahamas Defence spotter plane number one. Over."

"This is spotter plane one to *Intrepid*. Over."

"Spotter plane number one. What is your position? Over."

"Standby *Intrepid*."

Pembroke takes a breath to calm down and have patience. He figures correctly that the pilot is alone and is also serving as the navigator.

"*Intrepid*, we are sixty miles west of the tip of Andros Island, Bahamas. Over."

Pembroke lets out a sigh of relief. "Spotter one you are

beyond the middle of the Gulf Stream and therefore outside your jurisdiction. Over.

"*Intrepid.* The Government of the Commonwealth of the Bahamas Islands declared the spiny lobster a creature of the continental shelf. Over."

"Spotter one. That means the Bahamas claim all lobsters on their side of the Florida Straits. Your position is well on the U.S. side. Over."

"*Intrepid*, I beg to differ. Over."

"Spotter one: take it up with the American Ambassador. Out."

The church kitchen crowd listening to the radio conversation has swelled to standing room only. Upon hearing Pembroke's retort, they cheer in unison. Then Pastor Kenyon booms, "To the docks!"

The *Intrepid* slices the sea at full throttle, throwing a furiously wide bow spray toward what Pembroke figures is an intersecting course with the *Sonny Bays*. Pembroke studies the radar screen, noting several blips moving to the same common position.

Onboard the *Sonny Bays*, Randy Born rotates his stance as he captures another low altitude pass of the Bahamian plane. "Best one yet!" he enthusiastically shouts. The others lie low.

Catbait cackles, "Tink dats his last run, mon?"

Erric turns to Jack, "Hey, Jumping Jack Flashback, will this haunt you?" Jack manages a grin.

Captain Pembroke exits the wheelhouse of the *Intrepid* to stand on the deck and grimly inspects the *Sonny Bays* crew a short distance away. The men stand in a line along the gunnel facing the *Intrepid* as if they are under inspection by a drill sergeant. Pembroke raises a megaphone to his lips, "*Sonny Bays*, you didn't respond to my radio call."

Erric holds up the lifeless radio microphone by its cord above his head like a dead mouse. Pembroke's face remains stern. With his other hand, Erric grabs and twists Catbait's wrist to show the coffee cup is empty; in essence demonstrating exactly what had happened. Erric nods to the defunct microphone gently swinging by the cord.

Jack holds up a makeshift message scrawled on a burlap bag that reads, "No guns."

Pembroke's expression breaks into acknowledgement with a hint of a smile. He sees the flotilla of fishing boats bearing down on them from the horizon. He turns to the men of the *Sonny Bays* and gives them a crisp salute. The men return the gesture. Pembroke disappears inside the wheelhouse and addresses those in attendance, "As far as I'm concerned this never happened. Understood?"

"Yes, sir," the men respond resolutely.

"Besides," Pembroke smiles, "Can you imagine the paperwork we'd have to fill out?"

Erric, Rod, Jack, and Catbait wedge themselves into the *Sonny Bays* wheelhouse out of sight of Pembroke.

"To the best crew I've ever had," Erric slaps them on their backs as they whoop and holler.

"Would we be any other way, mon?" Catbait questions.

They return to the deck as the *Intrepid* peels away to run parallel with them at a reasonable distance. The friendly flotilla of fellow fishing vessels maneuvers to surround and accompany *Sonny Bays* towards the safety of Conch Key harbor.

Erric absently fingers the cross around his neck, feels a warm flush of resolution in his chest and whispers to himself, "Katherine."

Buried in thought, Jack comes to the surface piping up with, "Forget nightmares about the past. Living like this is exciting enough!" In response, Erric throws his head back and hoots.

On the Thorman pier, the jubilant church group gathers around a card table supporting Mamie's blaring marine radio. The celebration expands with the additions of Maria Gonzales and other fishermen's wives and children.

From the bridge of the *Intrepid*, Pembroke peers

through binoculars, keeping tabs on the *Sonny Bays*. He puzzles over Erric and Rod having a nose-to-nose conversation; Jack joins the two and almost immediately slaps Erric on the back.

Pembroke drops his field glasses, thinking to himself what more could these sometimes-devious friends be planning now?

The Coast Guard captain resumes his reconnaissance to see Randy Born grinding away on the action. Erric hails another boat to come alongside, takes a few steps back, makes a mighty running leap, and lands on the deck of the *Ponce de Leon*. After a hug from Javier, he shakes hands with the Gonzales sons.

Erric heads to the wheelhouse and lifts the radio microphone; Pembroke turns up his coast guard receiver volume.

Erric's excited voice echoes through radios up and down the Keys, "This is Erric Thorman on board the *Ponce de Leon* calling Thorman base, over."

"This is Thorman base," Mamie answers. "Over."

"Hey, Mom. Could you put Kath on the radio, please? Over" A surprised Katherine threads her way through the crowd which buzzes with anticipation. Attempting to remain cool despite her rising emotions, she casually intones, "This is Katherine Stillwell, over."

"I'm bringing your cross back like I promised. Over."

Nearly whispering, Katherine reacts, "Thank God you're okay, Ricky. I… I…"

From heaven's viewpoint, every person up and down the Keys listening to this transmission simultaneously moves closer to the radio as if they are all part of the same organism.

In a lowered voice, Erric tenderly answers, "Thanks, Kath." He drops his hand holding the mic and composes himself. A rallied Erric continues, "Hey, I talked to your dad. He says it's okay."

"What's okay, Ricky?"

Rick steels himself, "Katherine Stillwell, would you marry me?"

The dock is stone silent. "Yes," Katherine hoarsely whispers.

"Sorry, you broke up, Kath. What was that?"

"YES!" Katherine screams.

The crowd roars with joy. Mamie and Katherine hug wet cheek to wet cheek. They turn to see the *Ponce de Leon* rounding the turn into Conch Key harbor with the other boats on their tail. All the boat crews jump up and down shouting in glee across the water.

Katherine waves then grabs the mic, "Wait a minute, Erric! Don't you have something else to say to me?"

Erric struggles as he clasps the cross. Jack fingers his chaney.

Those on the dock strain to hear the response. Along with them others do the same on their marine radios in fishing boats, houses… everywhere up and down the keys.

Erric clears his throat, “This is Erric Thorman aboard the *Ponce de Leon* to Thorman base. Over.”

Katherine straightens up her blonde hair catching rays of the setting sun. She meets Erric’s formal tone, “This is Thorman base. Go ahead *Ponce de Leon*. Over.”

Erric grins broadly, “Katherine Stillwell, I’ve always loved you and will continue to love you forever. You’re my treasure. Out.”

The *Ponce de Leon* approaches the Thorman dock on the way to Stillwell Fisheries. Rod signals Javier and crew on the *Ponce de Leon* who laugh and shove Erric off the boat into the darkening water. Randy Born grins broadly; proud to have gotten this shot.

Jazzie, who knows Larry Beeker is watching her, turns and gives him an ever so subtle “maybe” smile with a raised eyebrow. Beeker sighs with a wry grin.

On the deck, Rod signals to Katherine for her to jump into the water. She obediently leaps into the harbor. Rod shouts to the dock, “Hey, Mamie. Glorious news, huh?”

Mamie radiates a warm smile. She touches her lips with an index finger, tosses this peck on the cheek kiss to Rod and drops her hand to her heart. Rod beams and turns away, pretending to be busy piloting the boat; he hides his misty eyes.

While swimming toward each other, Katherine dives below the surface. Erric laughs and shouts, "I know this game, Kath." He submerges and gives her a long embracing kiss under water until their lungs burn for air.

Jack watches the swirling water and bubbles sparkling gold in the fading light where his brother and Katherine hide their intimate display of affection. He straightens with an epiphany, then slowly smiles. "Goodbye yesterday," he announces to the heavens, and with all his strength throws his chaney far out in the harbor. After the splash he adds, "Hello God."

Erric and Katherine break the surface, draw several deep breaths, then submerge again to the cheers of those on the dock.

<•{{{><

Looking up from the sandy bottom, we see two bodies frolic together in silhouette against the brilliantly sparkling plain between the sea and air above.

A young boy and girl break the shimmering surface, laughing. In shallow water nearby, Erric puts his arm around Katherine as they watch the children at play this September day. "Twins! I still can't get over it," Erric brags.

"Don't forget I had something to do with it, too." Katherine teases. They laugh together. "My aunt Linda is a saint. She has taken care of the kids when I couldn't. I can never repay her."

They both fall silent for a moment, watching the children cavort in the water like two otters. Katherine fingers and then glances at her wedding ring sparkling in the sunlight. Erric turns to Katherine, "Did you hear people are sending mom checks?"

"Who? Why?"

"That follow-up story Fred Hammond did on us and the family. He mentioned mom needing an operation. People can really be generous."

"Really?"

"Yeah, we've got enough to pay for it."

Katherine hugs Erric, "I'm so happy for you all."

Erric adds, "It looks like there's enough left over to help with Rod's loan." Katherine giggles with delight. Erric continues, "Oh, I almost forgot," he removes the necklace from around his neck and offers it to her.

Katherine smiles warmly and gazes into his eyes, "No,

Erric. I want you to wear it forever to remind us what it took to get together again."

"Kath, I'll treasure it like I do you. To me you're worth more than all the gold in the Caribbean." He puts it back on and she lovingly strokes the crucifix.

"Spiritually, I think we were never apart, Kath." He gestures to the two children in the water, "Now we're a family. Who knew you could keep those two a secret?"

"It was for your own good," she assures him.

Erric places his hands firmly on her shoulders, brings her face to face and pretends to be alarmed, "Tell me you have no more deep secrets!"

They laugh heartily and turn to watch their children, who have adapted quickly to the warm, clear water of the Florida Keys.

Afterword

Over twenty years of writing and dreaming finally culminated in the publication of Traps.

It began as a movie script a few years before I accepted Jesus as my Savior in 1994. Buoyant in my new spiritual relationship I was topping the Sepulveda Pass on the 405-freeway heading north when the San Fernando Valley came into view. Remembering that this was the same place a pastor I knew would declare, "Devil, I've been out of town, but I'm back. Look out!" made me smile and admire his brave dedication. It gave me pause to consider my own purpose in this new life God had given to me.

I spoke out loud to Him, "Why am I on this earth? What am I supposed to do for You? Come to think of it, is this script I'm writing part of your plan?"

Although not audible to my ears, His still small voice replied, "Why don't you put *me* into the story?"

Over fifteen years later, the script expanded into a novella. I was designing a cover for *Traps* and gearing up to self-publish when I spotted an ad soliciting authors by CBN/Trilogy Publishing. I quickly discerned this event as God-arranged; confirmed by their acceptance of my manuscript.

Traps is based on true events: A lobster boat sneaked

into the newly declared Bahamian fishing waters, pulled their lobster traps, and suffered dive bombing passes from the Bahamian Coast Guard airplane as they charged back to the Florida Keys. On board were two co-worker friends of mine from WTVJ news. I gave the cameraman character my own attributes and thoughts based on my forty years plus of television production experience.

God willing, Randy Born, my cameraman alter ego character will continue in books yet to come.

Please pray for me,

Glenn “Kirk” Kirkpatrick

Appendix

• Lobster in the Florida Keys are also known as "bugs" because these crustaceans and insects are both invertebrates and come from the same phylum, Arthropoda.

• Lobster only became a delicacy in recent times. Lobsters were initially used as fertilizer in the fields or as bait for fishing. During our nation's early history Maine lobsters were harvested from tidal pools and considered "poverty food" fit only for minors, incarcerated prisoners, and indentured servants. In Massachusetts servants rebelled demanding that their contracts specify they would not be served lobster more than three times a week. Trapping lobsters began in the early 1800s.

• Spiny lobsters can grow to almost monstrous proportions. One record-breaking twenty-one pounder was estimated to be over twenty years old.

• Trapping lobster is only one modern method of acquiring these protein rich specimens.

- During daylight hours determined pleasure divers armed with heavy gloves and about a two-foot piece of angle iron or reinforcement rod, search rock crevices. The crustaceans sit head facing outwards. The hunter uses the metal rod as a "tickle stick" to reach into the hole behind the delectable creature to touch or tickle him out of his hideout. Gloves make grabbing the spiny shelled creatures more comfortable and thus practical. The creatures can be carried back to the boat in a porous gunny sack.

- At night tactics change. In a shallow draft boat or canoe shellfish hunters drift over grass flats with gasoline lanterns and focused beam spotlights looking for these night feeders. A "bully net" scoops up the lobster. A bully net positions the loop at a ninety-degree angle at the end of a long pole so the catcher can shove the net down on top of the prey; the lobster flees upward capturing itself in the net.

Note: Make sure your prime spotter understands that live lobsters are a mottled brownish green in color, otherwise you'll be scooping up Coca Cola cans which look like cooked lobster.

• Lobsters will sometimes migrate across the Florida Straits in long lines perhaps over fifty creatures in a single line. These sensitive animals navigate by smelling and tasting substances native to specific geographic areas of the ocean floor. Recent research reveals they also use the earth's magnetic field to find their way. Some have been tracked to find they can walk almost two miles a day across the bottom.

• The Caribbean spiny lobster, Panulirus argus, ranges from North Carolina to Brazil.

• Crayfish like spiny lobsters lack large claws to use as protection like their cold-water cousins. Instead warm water lobsters deter predators with a loud screeching sound made by rubbing their antennae against their bodies. Lobsters are social by nature, although some studies indicate healthy lobsters will avoid their diseased counterparts.

About the Author

Glenn "Kirk" Kirkpatrick grew up visiting his father on the set of various film productions. That exposure to the industry seeped into his spirit making any other vocation an almost impossible choice.

Kirk's career started in Florida news and documentaries, progressed to TV commercials in New York City and Atlanta and finally transitioned to reality TV in Los Angeles.

In the city of Angels, God powerfully spoke to Kirk of his future through Habakkuk 2:3,

"For the revelation awaits an appointed time;
it speaks of the end
and will not prove false.
Though it linger, wait for it;
it will certainly come
and will not delay."

Kirk printed the words over a blue sky and clouds posting it over his desk. He read this verse often knowing in his heart that he was to prepare for change.

A clerk at Lighthouse Christian Bookstore in L.A. pulled him aside to give him a word from God, "You will be joining a big company which needs you. You will be doing a lot of public speaking… without notes."

His wife's desire to join family in Utah convinced

him to go on a "scouting trip" to explore the possibility of moving there, but Kirk resisted since he wasn't sure it was God's plan.

In Sunday morning church service in Cedar City, Kirk was impacted by the minister's vision for multiplying thirty-two church plants. Kirk felt as though God was calling him to be a part of that mission. He shared the revelation with family commenting out loud, "But what will I do for a living? There's no television here in the desert."

God promptly assured him, "Kirk, my work is more important."

Kirk retired from television, moved to Utah and tried starting a number of second careers, until settling into the perfect job: leading tours around the Southwest. He works for a large company that needs him to drive a van and *speak, without notes,* to groups of tourists.

Kirk reflects upon the section of the above Habbakkuk passage, "Though it linger, wait for it;" and how the lingering story of *Traps* has finally become a reality.

CPSIA information can be obtained
at www.ICGtesting.com
Printed in the USA
BVHW041657150322
631532BV00012B/823